THE BIG BOSS

PENNY WYLDER

1

___

JUSTINE

This has been a shitty day.

I know that there are people who are definitely having a worse day than I am, but the black cloud hovering over my head shows no sign of clearing.

Of course the day I decide to do this favor is the day that I get caught in a freak rainstorm without an umbrella. My clothes are soaked and the air conditioning in this building is in overdrive thanks to the summer heat.

My shirt is way too thin for this, and my bra is completely visible. But in my defense, there was nothing in the weather forecast that called for rain today. Which is rare for Portland, and I was looking forward to enjoying it.

Next on the list of things that have darkened my mood, I was ogled in the elevator of this swanky office building by a tech bro in a suit who was yelling so loudly into his cellphone that his voice was echoing in the small space.

He looked like he'd never done a day's work in his life, and the way his gaze travelled over me made me colder than the air conditioning. Asshole. Just because you're wearing a

Rolex doesn't give you the right to look at me like I'm on display for your benefit.

And finally, now I'm standing in front of a set of double doors to a ridiculously ostentatious office because the secretary for Lila's client wouldn't take the damn flowers from me and told me to deliver them myself—all while looking at me like I'm a total street rat.

Even though I'm sure I do look like one. That much I'll give her. But seriously. They're flowers. Is it really that hard to get up and walk the extra fifty feet? I already brought them all the way here.

Taking a deep breath, I force myself to calm down. I'm doing this for Lila. It's not her fault that she got sick, and it's not her fault that this guy—Keenan Silverman—is one of her biggest clients. In fact, he's basically the reason her store is still afloat at all. And he's exacting. To a T. He's the kind of guy that wouldn't have any qualms about taking his business elsewhere if a delivery was delayed or missed—even if the proprietor was sick.

I would do anything for my friends. Especially Lila. Even brave the evils of corporate America to deliver weekly flowers to this snob of a businessman. And I loathe snobs. I really do. I prefer men who work for a living with their own hands and don't have a problem getting a little dirty.

Knocking on the door, I hear a muffled word to come in, and I'm faced with a man that is going to make me eat all my words. When Lila talked about Keenan Silverman, she described him as a Type A nightmare who wants everything done to perfection. He's a ruthless businessman at the top of his game. I didn't expect him to be barely over thirty years old.

The man in front of me could change the way I think about suits. Even sitting behind the massive desk with the phone to his ear, you can see that his suit is tailored for his body, and it's one hell of hell of a body. Everything about him drips wealth. His shoes alone probably cost more than my college degree. The one I'm still paying off one small payment at a time.

And if that isn't enough, he's gorgeous. Seriously fucking hot like he stepped off of some beach in Greece. Perfectly and lightly tanned even though we live in the Pacific Northwest, a jaw that could book him magazine ads with no trouble, and dark blue eyes that are mesmerizing even from across the room.

I realize that I'm standing half-way in the door, and he raises an eyebrow with a little smirk and gestures me into the room. There was a moment there when I opened the door that I was seriously regretting being a rain-soaked mess, but that smirk undoes all of that. Just because he's hot doesn't mean he isn't everything that Lila said he is. It's just in a beautiful package.

Fuck. Why are all the awful ones always gorgeous? I straighten my shoulders and march over to the desk and place the flowers down as he speaks into the phone. There. Job done. Lila will be happy. Her business is safe, and now I need to get myself some kind of endorphins. A cookie will do.

I turn to go and I hear the phone land in the cradle. "Where are you going?"

I freeze, realizing that he's talking to me. "I'm sorry?"

"I asked where you're going."

Turning back to him, I meet his eyes and ignore the thrill that runs down my spine. Down girl, he's not *that* hot. Except for the fact that he totally is. "I delivered your flowers, and now I'm going."

He smirks again. "My flower deliveries also come with consultations on the arrangement for the next day."

"As in *tomorrow*?" For some reason I was under the impression that Lila delivered to this guy once a week. If he gets fresh flowers every day, not only do I understand why she didn't want to lose his business, but why the secretary didn't want to bring them back. The arrangement I placed on his desk is *not* cheap. One more tick against him.

I love Lila, but these flowers aren't something he buys to enjoy. They're a power move. The fact that he can have flowers delivered fresh every day is a statement about his wealth, and I'm sure it's gotten around this building.

"Yes," he says coolly, "as in tomorrow. Is that a problem?"

"Of course not," I say. "Just unexpected."

He tilts his head, looking at me. The way he's taking me in makes me pause, like he's trying to figure me out like a puzzle. "How so?"

"These flowers are beautiful," I say. "And a lot of work went into arranging them. They won't be dead by tomorrow, and it seems a little silly to throw something away like that just because it's a day old."

One eyebrow rises in question. "You assume I throw them away? Maybe I take them home."

I roll my eyes. "You get a new full bouquet of flowers delivered to your office every day and you take them home? I don't think so. Whatever penthouse you've managed to makeover into your steel and glass bachelor pad would be drowning with flowers."

I bite my lips realizing that I've probably said far, far too much. I don't like this man. I don't like his wealth or what he does for a living. But I'm not here for me, I'm here for Lila. For her, I can keep my mouth shut.

Mr. Silverman stands and looks around his office with a

smile, making his gaze stop on the large glass windows and steel accents. "You're right," he says. "I don't bring them home. But they don't always go to waste. Sometimes my secretary takes them or they're moved to other places in the building. But I like something different and...stimulating every day. However, if something is particularly beautiful, I take them home."

He comes around the desk, eyes dragging down my body when he says that, and suddenly I think that he's no longer talking about the flowers on his desk. Is he...hitting on me? The very idea is laughable. I still have potting soil on my shirt from tripping in the shop picking up the flowers. There's a hole in the knee of my jeans, not to mention I'm soaked and my hair is a god-awful mess.

I don't usually care how I look or what other people think of me. But people like Keenan Silverman? They care about appearances. Clearly. Or day-old flowers wouldn't bother him. If someone as gorgeous as *him* is hitting on me, then something is wrong with that picture. But he's still looking at me with undisguised interest, and I hate the fact that I have butterflies in my stomach that are rapidly turning to heat. I clear my throat. "Maybe you should mix it up," I say. "Get a cactus or something."

There's that smirk again. It lodges itself under my skin where I can't ignore it. "Something prickly to remember you by?"

"Or to burst your ego," I mutter under my breath. And then that breath is entirely gone because he's stepped into my space.

"I happen to like thorny things. Things with edges are exciting. Interesting. Unique. Much more interesting than a daisy, which seems to be very easily ruined."

When his eyes move to the flowers on the desk, I can

suddenly catch my breath, and then I follow his gaze to the half-crushed daisy that he's referring to. *Shit.* I was so careful. That was one of the things Lila had told me; Mr. Silverman doesn't like when things are damaged.

"I apologize for the damage," I say, utterly resenting how breathless I sound. My body needs to get her shit together.

His eyes lock on mine again, such a peculiar and beautiful shade of blue. "I'll survive." Swiftly he turns back to his desk, and I don't dare move, because it doesn't feel like I can. A shuffle of papers and the scribble of a pen. When he turns back there's an envelope in his hand and that stupid, hot as fuck smirk on his face.

"What's this?"

"Payment."

"Oh." It's the only thing I can say, trapped by his gaze like I am. I thought that Lila had already been paid, but this is fine. "Thank you."

I need to get the fuck out of here. Being close to him is making my head spin and I'm too hot and too tempted for no goddamn reason. I barely get out the words "have a nice day," before I'm nearly sprinting out of his office and to the elevator. My heart is pounding and I'm out of breath.

What the fuck *was that*?

That was...nothing like I expected. At all. The door to the elevator closes behind me—thankfully I'm alone this time—and I open the envelope. Inside is a fifty-dollar bill and a note in flowing handwriting.

A tip for a memorable delivery experience. Thank Lila for me. Her business is proving to be a good investment in many ways.

   -K.S.

· · ·

Definitely not what I was expecting.

2

JUSTINE

"It's so ridiculous," I say under my breath as I pour water into a pan.

"It's really not," Lila counters again from the couch, coughing.

I roll my eyes while I'm still facing away and she can't see me. "As a tip that's like...beyond extravagant. Even for someone as rich as he is. I don't know if it's supposed to be a compliment or an insult. Is it a power move? To show me that he can afford anything? To intimidate me for crushing the damn flower? Still really sorry about that by the way. Is it like...a jab? Like 'I'm going to be generous and magnanimous to you even though you mouthed off to me'?"

I stop, and Lila coughs again. "You are seriously overthinking this, J. Maybe he just genuinely wanted to give you a tip. He wants new flowers every day, so he obviously values new experiences. I've been delivering to him for months."

"Exactly!" I yell, "And he's never given you a tip like this."

It's her turn to roll her eyes. "He always tips me, J. Not fifty, but he tips."

"I just don't get it." I keep my eyes on the pot and actually try to make it boil, unlike the saying. "And it's incredibly not okay that you didn't tell me how fucking hot he was."

"I mentioned it."

"Not like *that*. Not GQ model, please strip down for me now so I can worship your body *hot*."

I can tell by the look on Lila's face that she's holding back laughter. "What?"

She bursts out with it, holding her stomach and dissolving into coughs. "Oh my god, laughing hurts. Make it stop."

"I'm sorry. I wasn't trying to make you laugh."

"I know you weren't, but that doesn't mean it's not funny," she manages.

One by one, I start adding the ingredients to the home-made soup I'm preparing for her. It's one of my specialties. "Glad I can entertain you with my pain."

She coughs one more laugh. "Thank you for delivering the flowers. I really owe you one. Did he say what he wanted for tomorrow?"

"No," I shake my head.

"That's fine. He'll just email it to me."

I don't tell her about the whole cactus thing. Now I think that if I do, she might laugh at me. But all I feel when I look back on the whole encounter is...unsettled. I've never met a man that has so thoroughly managed to knock me off balance in such a short a time. And I can't even say *why* he was able to do it.

"He really got under your skin, didn't he?" Lila asks.

"Yeah."

She sits up higher on the couch and I can see her better from my place in the kitchen. "I expected part of it, but not this much."

"What do you mean?"

She smiles. "I mean, you don't exactly hide your disdain for the upper class. I mean that you're a woman who literally earns her living by helping elderly people. I don't think you even own a fancy dress. You were never going to be comfortable walking into a glossy high rise with people in suits milling around. But I didn't realize he would twist you up so much."

"It's fine…" I say. "I'm just—I'm not used to people doing that to me."

"Me either. You're Ms. Unshakeable."

I stick out my tongue at her. It's one of her older nicknames for me. Because she always tells me that nothing rattles me. I wish that were true. She doesn't realize that she's the rock that keeps me stable. Which is why I would do anything for her. Including delivering flowers to way-too-sexy suit-wearing businessmen.

"How's normal work?" Lila asks.

"Pretty good. Normal. No new clients lately."

She smiles. "And your favorite?"

"She's great. I get to see her tomorrow." Rose is my favorite person in the world except for Lila. She's in her eighties and still has more energy than I do. But she has trouble walking, and that's why we help her. Rose has an uncanny ability to see through every situation and give advice that you didn't even know that you needed. I joke with her all the time and tell her that she's a seer.

And I've noticed that she doesn't disagree. I don't believe in all that, but Rose would be the person to change my mind if anyone could. I think it's more that she's been around the block and nothing can phase her now. She's the true Ms. Unshakable.

The soup starts to simmer, so I clean up the kitchen a little bit.

"How many clients do you have tomorrow?"

"Two. Why?"

She grimaces. "I was wondering if you wanted to earn a bit more on top of that tip. I'll definitely be in tomorrow, but I could use the help."

"Sure. Both of my clients are early in the day so I can be there by mid-morning."

"Thank you. I really appreciate it."

I laugh. "It's not a problem. But really Lila, you need to hire someone to help you. I don't mind doing it—you know I don't—but sick days happen, and you've got enough business that you could use an assistant." It was lucky that she got sick when she did. She was able to have the weekend off and take off today. One day lost instead of three. Small favors. She brings in someone a couple days a week for a few hours to lessen the load, but it's just not enough.

"Yeah," she sighs. We've had this conversation before. "I know. I want to look into it in a few months when I have more cover. If Silverman stays my client, then I will definitely be able to bring someone on. The amount of money he pays is *that* good."

"So he's pretty important to your future?"

"Yup."

I shake my head. "I'm really glad that you didn't tell me that before I went today. It probably would have been worse. I might have vomited on his floor."

Lila waves a hand. "It's fine, you're fine. He can be an exacting client, but he's still human. And every human makes mistakes."

Keenan Silverman doesn't seem like the kind of man that makes mistakes to me. Or tolerates them. The only reason I think we're in the clear is because of the note. He wouldn't have said that her business was a good investment if he was going to fire her tomorrow. That's good news at the very least.

Wandering around, I start to tidy. It's a habit when I'm anxious or my brain won't slow down. And with Lila's sickness, there's plenty to clean. She laughs softly as I attack the pile of magazines she's been working through. They're spilled off the coffee table and onto the floor. There's more than a few that have ads on the back—cologne ads featuring ripped men staring out of the pages trying to entice people.

Normally, it would work. But right now all I can think about is the fact that none to them hold a candle to Keenan Silverman, and I haven't even seen his body. I don't need to. He's hotter than them, hands down.

A blush rises up my chest onto my cheeks, and I shove him out of my mind. He shouldn't be in there at all. He was entitled and snobbish and just...*ugh.*

I set the magazines down in a stack a little too hard. Lila's eyes go wide. "You okay?"

"Fine," I say, smiling. Just plagued by the memories of the most confusing encounter I've ever had. Thankfully when I look at the stove, I see steam rising from the pot. "Soup is boiling."

"It smells amazing," Lila admits.

"It will be!"

Moving to check the soup, I shove Keenan out of my mind. He's just a hot guy. Nothing more. He's entitled, rich, and selfish. Just because Lila needs him doesn't mean I do, and I don't ever want to see him again.

3

KEENAN

I want to see her again.

That's the thought that's been plaguing my brain ever since she practically sprinted out of my office. Every time my eyes land on that damned bouquet that's sitting on my desk.

It's long past quitting time, but I can't leave yet. Too much to do, and that's not being helped by distracting memories. Might as well relax a little at least.

I cross over to the bar and pour myself a glass of whiskey. Smooth smoke on my tongue. Just the cost of this glass is more than some people's yearly salary. But I only tolerate the best in everything I do, and I have accomplished that with my business. So now I can afford luxuries like this whiskey.

The flowers catch my eyes again, especially that broken daisy. Normally I would be furious about the damage, but that mark...it was proof that she was standing here. I sigh as I return to the papers on my desk. Plans for a new development in the city, but there are logjams we have to work through. Permits. Demolition. More permits. Supply chains.

More permits. Construction. Not the world's most exciting evening. But it has to be done.

I'm sure if she were here it would be much more interesting. She was fire that I wanted to let burn me. She was defiant and open—something that I rarely see every day. I'm not used to anyone showing their authentic feelings to me. I'm the boss. The billionaire. Everyone needs or wants something from me, and disagreeing with me is never the way to get it.

Or so they think.

Her obvious disdain for me and my wealth is refreshing. Enticing. I want more of it. To hear the story of why she hates it. Because she must have a reason. Most people do.

The phone on my desk rings, and I sigh. It's Brandon, I can guarantee it. One of the only people who would call me right now. He's looking at the same documents on his desk.

"Hey Brandon."

"You knew it was me?" He sounds amused.

I chuckle and take a sip of my whiskey as I sit at my desk. "It's Monday and we're both workaholics. Of course I knew that it was you."

He laughs before clearing his throat. "Just looking over the plans for the development. Do you think we're going to get pushback?"

I frown. "Why would we?"

"There will be some displacement. Losing greenspace. To be clear, I don't think we should stop or anything, just wondering if you think they'll put up a fight."

I search until I find the paper with the more detailed plans for the development. We're demolishing an old building. Pre-1900. I've seen it, and it's pretty. We considered converting it, but it would cost more to convert it than it's worth. Starting fresh is faster. A small park is also going to be taken over. "I think it's fine," I say. "The numbers all add up, it will benefit the local community. And the residents were all compensated well."

"Some of these preservation groups don't always listen to that kind of logic." He sounds worried.

"What's going on?"

Brandon makes a sound of uncertainty. "Nothing for certain. Just some rumors that one of those groups is going to start targeting our projects. Again, not a reason to stop, but it's something to be aware of."

"Fair enough," I say. "Hopefully this one will be too fast for them to organize anything. Demo is scheduled for two weeks, provided the permits go through. And I'm having Marcy push them through tomorrow."

"Good," Brandon says. "I'll let you know if I hear anything else."

"Please do," I say, laughing. "Now go the fuck home."

"Only if you do."

We both know that neither of us is leaving the office anytime soon. But oh, I wish that I could. Because that damned daisy catches my eye again and I'm trapped in the circle of thoughts about the girl. And the fact that I'm an idiot and I didn't even get her name.

All I'm left with is the perfect image of her. Soaking wet and looking angry as all hell. I'm not sure why I find it so alluring, but I do. I can't remember the last time that someone came into my office angry. Usually people appear with masks of perfect pleasantness, hoping to charm me.

Her thin t-shirt showed every line of her generous curves and the bra I wasn't sure she meant to be on display. I wished I had been able to see it in more detail.

I wanted to see every part of her in more detail, from the way her face twisted in disdain to the way her lips parted when she didn't realize she was staring. I saw the curiosity, desire, and excitement hinted at in those gorgeous green eyes. She seemed to be out of breath, and I could only hope that it had something to do with me.

Fuck, I'm not getting anything done, and now I'm hard thinking about her. I need to see her again. There's no question. It should be easy enough, given her employer. My mind is already making the plans.

My entire life I've worked toward what I wanted. Laser focused. The office around me and the house that I own, and all the rich luxury that she seems to loathe are all results of my ambition. I pursue what I want. I reach all my goals. And my current goal is to see her again.

Because there's something between us, and feeling that so quickly is a rarity. Yeah, I'm going to see her again. This time I'm going to find out her name. And I'm going to show her that all the things that come with this life aren't so bad.

4

JUSTINE

I groan as I round the stairway on the fourth floor. These older buildings don't have elevators, and sometimes the grocery loads we have to carry are a bit too heavy for jogging up so many steps. And I can't leave the bags sitting on the sidewalk because they'll get snatched. I made that mistake once. Never again.

So now if it's too heavy, I ferry them inside and then do it in parts, half the load up one set of stairs to drop them at the landing. I end up getting a full workout every time I do it, but it's worth it for my clients. A lot of them are homebound with health problems, and the only way they get groceries is through me.

It's worth a little bit of sweat.

Especially for Rose.

Finally, I drag the last of the of the bags to her door and knock.

"It's already open, honey."

Rose is in the kitchen when I open the door. Her walker is next to her, and she's got a cup of tea for each of us ready to go. Like the badass she is. "How are you doing, Rose?"

"I'm fine—" She looks at me. "Maybe I should have made iced tea today, looking at that load."

I smile. "Nah. That looks great. It's just a little hot out there. The weather can't make up its mind."

Lugging the rest of the bags in to blessed air conditioning, I get started putting the cold stuff away before it all completely melts. And then the rest of it. "You sure you don't need help?" Rose asks, already sitting down at the table. She says it sarcastically because every time she asks me, I vehemently tell her no, that this is what I get paid for. She still asks now, but with a smirk on her face because she already knows what's going to happen and what I'm going to say.

"What tea do we have today?"

"Mint. I felt like something lighter was in order."

"Sounds yummy."

I finish putting the groceries away just the way that she likes them and then flop into the chair across from her.

"You work too hard, you know that?"

"On the contrary," I smile. "I think I work the exact right amount."

Rose rolls her eyes. "You say that now, but you'll get to be my age and think that you should have worked a little less and lived a little more. You're still doing all that activism stuff?"

I raise an eyebrow and add a little sugar to my tea. "Well, for now I'm fine. And yeah, got some of that coming up this week."

Rose looks at me closely. The woman misses nothing, and is sharper than any ten people that I've met put together. She's my favorite, but all my clients are like her. Hidden gems forgotten by the busy bustle of a city increasingly obsessed with luxury and money and everything that's *new*.

It makes me sad. What are we all missing by just continually going to the next thing and the next thing and the next instead of slowing down and enjoying the world a little bit? The stories I've heard from Rose and my other clients are worth far more than I could earn with a much larger paycheck at some corporate job.

I've always known that I wouldn't be happy in those circles. Helping people and standing up for what matters is where I've always been the happiest. And I'm pretty sure that it always will be.

"You're different today," Rose says.

I tilt my head. "Why do you say that? I don't feel different."

"No, you are," she says. "Your energy has shifted." There's a long pause, and then her eyes go wide. "You met someone."

"What?" My response is way more shrill than I would like. "No, I didn't. I mean, yes, I did. But trust me when I say that he's not the type of man that you would approve of."

Rose smirks. "Try me."

So I do. I tell her all about the encounter with Keenan in his office and his frustrating wealth and ridiculous attraction and the fucking chemistry that still bothers me. I shouldn't have any chemistry with someone like that. And how I don't understand why he would give me that kind of tip as anything other than an insult.

When I'm done, my friend is just looking at me and sipping her tea. After a moment, she says, "You should fuck him."

I nearly choke on the sip of mint I'd just taken. "Oh my god, Rose. You're trying to kill me. What? No!"

"Why not? You said it yourself that you're attracted to him."

I make a face. "He's everything that I stand against. I met him for five minutes, and I'll never see him again. Was he hot? Yes. But I don't need anything more than that. There are plenty of hot men in the world that aren't him."

"But chemistry like that is hard to come by, trust me. I'm not saying you have to date him, but if there are that many sparks flying between you, do yourself a favor and fuck him out of your system."

I sit there for a moment, completely stunned. Rose is witty and sharp and fierce, and I have *never* seen this side of her before. It takes a few moments of me frozen in utter shock before she starts laughing. "My god, Justine, don't act like I'm a sexless nun. I've got children. How do you think I got them?"

I laugh. "I know, I just wasn't expecting you to tell me to fuck someone today."

"No matter your principals, Justine, there is a shortage of truly excellent cock in this world. If you have the chance for it, take it and don't look back. You won't regret it later."

Taking another sip of my tea, I laugh again. "I'll keep that in mind. Though I'm dying to know what story you're going to drop on me that proves the point."

"A lady never kisses and tells," she says with a grin. "But she does swallow and spill. There are more than I think you have time for today, dear. But I remember once upon at a time at one of those parties that everyone talks about—you know, ballgowns and tiaras and all that—I was invited, who knows why." She stands and takes her cup to the sink slowly, another tradition of ours because she won't let me do it for her.

This isn't the first time that Rose has hinted at the fact that she had a glamourous life. It makes me wonder what her real story is and how she ended up here. She seems happy with where she is, and every time I try to ask her directly about her past, she shuts me down. But there are hints. Despite the age of this building, it's beautiful and vintage and I have no doubt that it costs an absolute shit-ton to live here. Not to mention the services she pays for, like me.

"Anyway," she continues, "we were dancing and drinking, and I saw this man across the room. Tall and blond and built—you know the type. And I swear that that man's eyes set me on fire. It only took a few minutes before he was crawling under my skirt and giving me one of the best orgasms of my life. We left the party and didn't look back. A night of some of the best cock I've ever had was well worth some dancing," she chuckled to herself. "I didn't find out till later that he was royalty. If I'd known, maybe I would have kept him another night."

"Rose, *oh my god*. Talk about burying the lede here. Royalty from *where?*"

She waves a hand. "That doesn't matter. The point is that you should enjoy yourself. Now come here, I have something for you."

"That's all you're going to give me?" I ask, pouting. "Really?"

"I could give you more details about the sex and the fact that his tongue was like a goddamn hurricane, but I don't think you want to hear about an old woman's love life."

I'm still tripping over the fact that she had a one-night stand with someone royal. That's so cool. And I'm sure she's concealing a lot of the juicy details. But if she thinks that I'm going to forget and not ask again, she's dead wrong. I down the rest of my tea and load my cup into the dishwasher before following her over to her guest room.

"One of my downstairs neighbors passed," she says.

"And they were giving away her things. I thought of your friend with the flower shop, thought she could use them."

"I'm sorry," I say. I didn't realize she'd had a neighbor that died.

Rose waves a hand. "She lived a long life, and we all knew it was coming. Went peacefully, and you would have liked her. But she would have smacked us both for being sad about it. I'm sorry I can't lift this."

I step around her and find a box on the floor. It's filled with absolutely stunning flower pots. Some hand crafted and painted, and immediately I know that Rose is right. Lila will love these. "Are you sure? These are really beautiful. I could help you plant some herbs in your window."

"No, thank you. I've got enough hobbies, and the flowers you bring me are as much as I can handle keeping alive."

"Fair enough," I say, laughing. The box is pretty heavy, but I can lift it. I'm glad I have my car with me today. On days with lighter loads, I'll sometimes take my bike. But I wasn't sure if Lila was going to need me to make deliveries today, and I had plenty to deliver to Rose anyway. Glancing at my phone, I wince. "I wish I could stay a little longer and make you tell me more about Mr. Royal, but I actually promised Lila that I would help her out at the store today."

"Oh, don't worry about me, honey. It's just nice to see you every week."

"Call me if you need anything, okay?"

"I will." She's never called me though, even though the post-it note with my cell number is still stuck on the fridge where I can see it. I would stay longer if I hadn't promised Lila. Maybe I'll drop by later this week and make sure that she's doing okay.

Carrying the pots down the stairs make me incredibly

grateful that Lila's shop is on the ground floor. She must have had whoever was helping clean her friend's apartment carry them up to hers.

It's not that far of a drive to the flower shop, and I'm right on time. It's only ten-thirty. Perfectly mid-morning. But when I walk in, I hear a shriek. "Oh thank *fuck* you're here," Lila says, running over to me and grabbing my arm, which nearly makes me drop the pots.

"Holy shit, slow down woman. What's going on?"

"I need your help," she says. "What are those?"

"Rose gave them to me for you."

Her eyes go huge and round. "They're beautiful!"

She tries to take them from me and I stop her. "You're still barely recovered. I've got them. Tell me why you're screaming?"

Jess—Lila's part-time employee—sticks her head out of the back. "She's freaking out about Mr. Silverman."

I put the pots down in a corner and turn to face my best friend. "What the hell did he do now?"

She presses her lips together and looks nervous. Her hands are fidgeting. "Really, Lila, is it that bad?"

"It's just weird, okay? He didn't order flowers. Normally he orders flowers. Big bouquets like the one you took over yesterday. But today he ordered...a cactus. Just one. Like... that's it. Just a cactus plant."

Oh shit.

"And it's not just that," she says. "He wants you to deliver it. Based on his note, it seems like he wants you to do all his deliveries from now on. I guess he thinks you work here? I had a small panic attack about the cactus because it was so different, but if he wants more deliveries, that means he's not just buying the cactus as a farewell purchase."

That fucking asshole. He didn't have enough playtime with me yesterday so now he wants more? And to think that he can just *demand* my time like he owns it makes me want to slap his stupidly handsome face. In fact, maybe I'll do just that after I give him a piece of my mind.

But on the other hand, he did take my advice. So he was listening to me. It was a small thing, but it was something.

"The cactus is my fault," I say. "Not yours. I suggested that he get something sharp so that he could deflate his ego."

Behind me, Jess bursts out laughing. "Oh my god, that's fucking hilarious. I would have paid money to see the look on his face."

Lila looks amused too. "I guess that's better than him just being tired of my arrangements," she says. "I'll get the cactus ready."

"Yeah," I say. "Give it to me. I'll take it to him as *his lordship* demands and tell him that he can't just assume everyone who walks into his office is a servant. I can't believe he just assumed who I was and where I worked."

Lila's face falls, and my stomach clenches. Fuck.

"Because working for me would be so terrible?"

"Jesus, Lila, that's not what I meant at all. You know I love being here and helping you, this is about a man who has too much money for his own damn good assuming that everyone else is beneath him. It has nothing to do with you."

She sighs. "You're right, I'm sorry. It's just…"

"I get it," I say. "He's an important client. I won't fuck up your relationship."

"Thanks." Lila smiles and gives me a hug before heading to grab the cactus.

And I will do that. I'm not going to fuck over my friend's

livelihood because some corporate billionaire is an asshole. But I'm going to make it clear what he can and cannot do while making assumptions about people he doesn't know. That much is for damn sure.

5

KEENAN

I can't focus on anything. This morning has been a complete loss waiting for the damn flower delivery. Or cactus delivery as today's case may be. I made it clear to Lila that I wanted the new girl to make the deliveries from now on, but it's possible that she might not be available.

My entire body seems to be buzzing with energy. I can barely explain it, but every nerve is electrified waiting to see her, this nameless woman that's taken hold of my imagination. I dreamed about her last night. Wanton, sexy dreams that had me out of bed and into the shower an hour earlier than normal just so I could jerk off.

More than once.

This limbo is maddening. This is why I try not to take chances with anything. Not in business, not in life. Chances mean there are possibilities for failure, and I don't like that. This whole morning has been maddening with the idea that she might not show up. And equally maddening with the idea that she will.

What will I say to her? "I'm drawn to you so impossibly and completely that I changed my entire routine to see you again?" That would sound at best desperate, and at worst entirely creepy.

It's a good thing that I didn't ask for her name because I would have tried to look her up last night, and that would be even more creepy. I just want to see her again to see if the chemistry that I felt is real, and if it's something that we should pursue. My gut tells me that it is. I've never felt anything like that before. Like lightning arcing between us.

I want to know everything about her.

There's a knock at the door, and *she* doesn't wait for me to respond before she enters, cactus in hand. And immediately she's talking even though she's pointedly not looking at me.

"Listen, you're an important client to Lila, and that's the only reason that I'm not screaming at you right now. But you have a lot of nerve ordering me here like I'm some kind of servant. I actually don't work for Lila. I'm her best friend and delivered your damn flowers yesterday because she was sick. I have my own job to worry about, let alone being bossed around by someone who thinks that he's better than everybody else."

She puts the cactus down on the desk a little too hard, and I don't even care. I'm drinking her in. Her hair cascades around her shoulder in dark waves, and her simple casual clothes highlight her form in a way that I hadn't appreciated before. She's definitely not the kind of woman I've tangled with in the past. And maybe that's the problem. Maybe that's exactly what I need.

I stand up, trying to hold back the smile from my face. Her anger at me is a bit justified, and a bit not. But I like the irreverence. I miss it. Crave it. "If you're going to tear me a new one, you should at least look me in the eye while you're doing it."

I don't care about the argument, but I want to see her eyes. That spark and fire that I can feel burning in my veins. She doesn't look at me, so I circle the desk to her, the need to be close nearly impossible to resist, and I'm barely holding my body in check. "If you want to scream at me, scream," I say. "I promise the soundproofing in here is good enough."

The innuendo is intentional, and she lifts her eyes to mine. Immediately the air in the room feels electric, and I know that she feels it too. This close, I can see the way her pupils dilate. This connection between us is raw and real, and like nothing I've ever felt.

"What's your name?" I ask softly.

"Justine." There's that breathlessness again. The sign I'm hoping means that this is just as overwhelming for her.

"Well, Justine, you were right. The cactus is a good choice. It's something I'll take home with me." I see her swallow, like she doesn't know what to say. Like she didn't expect this kind of response. "And I'm sorry that I offended you by assuming you worked for Lila. I would like to know more about you so I don't make that mistake again."

Anger suddenly flares in her eyes. "Are you toying with me?"

I do smile now. "No, I'm not."

"You must think I'm some kind of circus act or something parading around for your amusement. Or someone that you can walk all over. I know men like you. Obsessed with status and wealth and the size of their *office* and their bank account. You're not interested in me. Not really. I'm too down to earth for you. I'm nothing more than something different. A new flavor. That's it. You can't change my mind and I'm not fooled."

She raises her hand like she's thinking about slapping

me, and I catch her wrist. For a moment, my gaze focuses on her hand. There's dirt there—maybe from working with the flowers. And calluses. She's worked hard.

Looking back, her eyes are wide open on mine, and none of the anger that was there just seconds before is visible. Justine's chest rises and falls faster. She's right here with me in this moment, and it feels like we're hanging in the balance. We're going to fall one way or another. I want to fall into her.

"You're right," I say quietly. "Nothing I say right now will change your mind."

She makes a small sound, maybe a word, but I don't hear it because I am already kissing her. Nothing I said would have convinced her. Maybe my actions will. There was nothing in the world that could have kept me from kissing her, and as soon as our lips meet, the world explodes into fire and color.

Justine comes alive in my arms, kissing me back. A groan is torn from my throat. She tastes like mint and strawberries and everything sweet. But more than that, that undercurrent of electric fire.

Our tongues tangle together, and I'm blind with it. My cock is so hard that it's aching even after coming twice this morning with thoughts of her mouth. I need her. A blind need driven by passion and connection that I can't name.

We barely rise for breath. "Someone will come in," she says.

"Not a problem." I don't stop kissing her as I move her across the room, flipping the lock on the door before pinning her against it. I run my hands down her curves and she moans into my mouth. Just that sound drives all the rest of my blood south. I want to hear it again, and louder.

I wasn't joking. This office is perfectly sound-proofed. It

was designed to be protective of sensitive phone calls, but it will work equally as well now.

Justine's body is soft against mine, and I press my hips into hers. She gasps under my mouth, eyes suddenly flying wide as she feels my erection. God, yes. Everything about her is open and vulnerable and hungry. I want to taste her. Be inside of her. Consume her.

I kiss her again, running my tongue along her lips until she opens and surrenders again, exploring every inch of her that I can reach. But Justine is exploring too, and I have to break off our kiss when she touches my cock. Even through my pants, I see white.

Fucking hell, I need to inside her.

"Yes," she breathes, and I realize with shock that I whispered the words. *I need to be inside you*. And she said yes.

My brain is an entirely different kind of blank as I haul her off her feet and into my arms. I carry her across to the desk and set her on top of it, only to hear too late the sound of scraping. I lunge for the cactus and catch it, luckily not impaling myself on the spines. Even if nothing else happens between us, I need it as a reminder that she is real. That it happened.

Setting the cactus aside, I catch Justine watching me. Her eyes are still wide and dark, but I can't help but wonder what she thinks of me saving the plant that she told me to buy out of spite. And I can barely believe that I already have an attachment to the tiny green thing.

And then I don't care, because she spreads her legs. Even still clothed, it's an invitation. One that I take. I consume her mouth again, this time lifting her shirt over her head and tossing it aside. Her bra follows along with my suit jacket, and I stop her from unbuttoning my shirt to taste her perfect pink nipples, already hard under my tongue.

I savor the tiny moan that breaks away from her when I suck harder, for a moment wishing that I could take my time and worship this woman with everything that I have. But we're far too desperate for that.

Stripping off my shirt, I undo my belt and shove my pants down while Justine does the same. I grab the condom from my wallet and stroke it on, gritting my teeth. I'm so hard that I feel like a goddamn teenager about to blow his load.

Justine's pussy is glistening between her spread legs, so wet and inviting. I don't think that I've ever seen anything that hot. Reaching out, I hold both sides of her face, kissing her as gently as I'm able before it once again dissolves into nothing but us clawing for more.

"You want this?" I gasp.

"Yes," Justine moans. "Fuck me, Keenan."

I don't wait for her to tell me twice, I just kiss her, bearing her back until she's flat on the desk and my cock is pressing against her heat. I line myself up against her before sinking in, and it's like heaven. Pure pleasure and need spiraling through me.

I will never be the same.

6

JUSTINE

Keenan slams home in one stroke, and I fall apart. This isn't normal sex or a random hook-up. This feels like the coming together of two people who have been wanting each other and denied for years. Not two total strangers who met *yesterday*.

When he touched me I swore it was like two magnets pulling us together, and I knew that I was fucked, both literally and figuratively. There wasn't any turning back. All I could think about was Rose and the way she told me to go for it.

I can't explain the connection between us. It's why I didn't look at him when I first came into his office today. As soon as I saw him, everything snapped into focus, and I was done for. Now I'm on his desk, wetter than I've ever been in my life, and oh *god* he feels so fucking good.

This is hard and fast and exactly what I need. I want more. I want it all. I want fast and slow and to explore everything that he can make me feel. Just his lips on my skin has me ready to come and I'm almost there now, biting my lip to keep myself from screaming.

Keenan has a perfect, gorgeous rhythm, and I can barely see straight through the haze of pleasure flowing in through everything. I can see him over me, and through that delicious haze I realize that I was right. He has the body of a god, perfectly toned in all the right places, muscles tensing and releasing as he fucks me with brutal force.

Pleasure gathers at my core, deep at the center in that place where his cock is reaching. He's the perfect length for me, filling me up and stretching me full without any pain. Just decadent ecstasy that's galloping at a million miles a minute.

Keenan pulls back, standing straight and placing a hand on my chest, holding me in place as he works me with fast, hard strokes. I close my eyes, bathing in the pleasure.

"Let me hear you," he growls, voice low and desperate. "No one else can."

I don't want to scream. It feels too fast and too vulnerable and too much of everything, but he shifts the angle of his hips and I lose control of my voice, a moan slipping past my lips.

"More."

Everything coalesces as he drives into me, compressing and then exploding into nothing but light and sheer, utter bliss. I know I scream. I've always been loud in bed and this is the best sex that I've ever had.

The pleasure rolls across my skin and sinks through it. The world fades to nothing but the movement of Keenan's body as I ride out the orgasm. I'm blind with it. Shaking, groaning, begging. And then he's gone.

He's pulled out of me entirely, and I open my eyes to nothing. Keenan isn't standing there anymore...because his head is between my legs, tongue tasting my orgasm, dipping inside the space his cock just left. He groans. "You're delicious."

"Fuck," I say, covering my face with my hands. My body jumps in spasms, already overloaded with every kind of sensation, but he doesn't stop, dipping and swirling his tongue up and over my clit until I'm once again on the edge of pleasure, so perfect that I can nearly taste it in the air.

I reach out, burying my hands in his hair and pulling him closer before he pulls away with a feral grin and shining lips. He fits the head of his cock against me and thrusts once, burying himself deep. So deep it sends me over in one go, and I fall into the second wave of pleasure.

This time I'm not entirely sure that I'll come back up. His own efforts are hard and fast, and I feel it when he comes, rhythm faltering enough that he has to brace himself on the desk above me. One more thrust, and again, and he cries out his pleasure before going still.

We both collapse into silence, hanging in the aftermath together. The air is thick with the scent of us together—and just of him. Rich leather and cedar.

What the fuck just happened?

I feel like I'm coming out of a trance as I look up at him, breathing hard above me. He is so fucking beautiful, and he is still *inside me*. Oh my god. I must have lost my mind.

This wasn't why I came here today. I came here to preserve Lila's business relationship and tell him what a vile, despicable human being he is. And I let him fuck me on his desk.

And deep in my gut I know that if he turned me over and took me from behind, I wouldn't say no. I squeeze down on his cock inside me and watch as those already dark blue eyes grow darker again. One eyebrow rises. "Do you want more?"

Yes. Fuck yes.

But I don't speak those words. I just stare at him for a moment, and slowly, he slips out of me and away. I hear his voice speaking but I can't focus on his words. Everything is distant. I can't seem to make sense of any of it.

I'm no prude. I love sex, but this—this isn't something I normally do. Ever. Do I regret it?

No.

Rose was right, I won't ever regret it. I can't. It was too good and too perfect and everything inside me feels calmer. I wish that it just wasn't with *Keenan Silverman*. I did more research on him, and he's exactly the type of person that I need to stay away from. Overwhelmingly rich, cocky, and everything that comes along with that.

Glancing over, he's silhouetted against the windows as he dresses, and I get a glimpse of a perfectly muscled back and a tattoo. A gorgeously rendered flock of birds swooping across from one shoulder to the other. They disappear as he shrugs the shirt over his shoulders.

"Justine?"

I shake my head. "Yeah?"

He smiles. "Did you hear what I asked?"

Biting my lip, I shake my head.

"I asked if you wanted to go to dinner with me tonight."

Suddenly everything shifts. I feel exposed and bare—which I am. I slip off the desk and pull up my underwear and jeans, redoing my belt before hunting for my bra and finding my shirt. I'm not a self-conscious person by any means, but now I feel out of place. Shabby in comparison to everything shiny in this office. Even the desk that he just fucked me on. Everything I'm wearing is...normal for me. Plain underwear and fraying pants. Second-hand t-shirt.

How could I possibly go anywhere with him? I barely fit

into his office here, if I showed up at some fancy restaurant I would be laughed out without a second thought. I'm sure that the offer to take me out is genuine—I know that he can feel this thing between us as well as I can, but we're from two completely different worlds. And sadly, I can't ignore that.

"I—" The words on my lips are about to be an excuse. Some lie about how I have to help Lila again or that I have a late client to see, but they stop dead on my lips. After what we just happened—what we shared—it feels wrong to lie to him.

My eyes catch on the cactus at the edge of the desk. He practically dived to the ground to save it. I straighten it so it looks better, and give him a small, polite smile. "I'm sorry, but I can't."

"Why not?" `

"I just...I can't see you again," I say firmly, even though I'm regretting the words as I'm saying them. But it doesn't make them any less true. "Especially not in public. You are who you are, Keenan. You're from this world. You belong in your thousand-dollar suits and among your daily fresh flowers. You're everything that I'm not.

"And even if that weren't a problem, the very thing that I do is basically stand against you every day. You're the kind of person that makes my life difficult. You wanted to know what I do? I work for a non-profit that assists elderly people. People forgotten because their neighborhoods are changing so much that people don't even notice when they need help. Because they're all filled with luxury apartments and high rises and people who are too rich to fucking care that their neighbors can't walk down the stairs for groceries. All thanks to people like you.

"I know what you do," I say, ending my sudden rant with

a release of breath. I didn't expect for that to all come out at once. I wasn't planning on it at all. *Shit*. I didn't actually want to insult him that much. Especially because of Lila.

But he doesn't look insulted. He barely looks phased. Just assessing me with a cool glance as if he hadn't just fucked the shit out of me five minutes ago.

"So," I say. "Thank you, but—"

"Thank you for what?" he asks with that devastating smirk. "The sex?"

A blush creeps up my cheeks. I guess that is what I am thanking him for. "Goodbye, Mr. Silverman."

I make it halfway to the door before I hear his voice behind me. "I think you're making a lot of assumptions about me, Justine."

The words make me pause, and I stop. But I don't turn around. Because looking at him does strange things to me that I can't explain. I think he's going to say something else to convince me, but he doesn't. And he probably won't. He's just like the rest of them. Like all the politicians and CEOs that have promised that they're different and that they'll actually change. But they never do. It's not who they are. Money will always win out for people like him.

My work and my ethics are too important to me to sacrifice by jumping in bed with the enemy. Even if every second of that would be filled with pleasure.

Keenan doesn't speak, and I walk away before I can't make myself leave.

7

JUSTINE

I really need to get out of here. Because I feel like I'm walking away from something I shouldn't be, even if I *know* that I'm right. But I force myself to walk at a normal pace past his secretary to the elevator.

He's on my skin. I can feel him and smell him. That alluring combination of cedar and leather. It's like it's walking with me in a cloud, reminding me of pleasure and passion and everything else.

I want to get him out of my nose so badly that I scrub at my face, which of course doesn't work. It's partly his cologne, and partly just a mark he left on me. By being in me. By tasting me.

The elevator seems like it's moving in slow motion, I swear. My car is parked a couple of blocks away. I need to get there so I can go home and shower and put Keenan Silverman out of my mind.

Rose's advice was solid. I don't regret a single second of that experience. But it would take a lot more than being taken on a desk to fuck that man out of my system. And it would be enough to suck me in and make him truly dangerous. Getting used to him—to that kind of life and what it can mean...

It's terrifying. I don't want to lose the sense of who I am, and I feel like Keenan is the kind of man that has the potential to make me forget absolutely everything. *Everything.*

What they don't tell you about really great dick, is that it's addictive. You always want more until you want nothing else. And that's the beginning of the end.

The sun is still shining hot and bright, and the humidity instantly makes me sweat. And that only helps me remember more, smell him more. What the fuck am I doing?

I look to my right as I step onto the street, and suddenly there's blaring horns and a rush of air and I'm falling on top of someone's body. The wind is entirely knocked out of me, and my vision blackens with dizziness for a moment before it clears and I'm looking up at the sky.

Running through the images in my head, I realize how close I'd just come to that bumper, and the rush of wind was the car that nearly killed me.

A face blocks out the sun. "Justine." It's Keenan. "Are you all right? Did you hit anything?"

I try to focus on his voice. "I landed on you."

"Good. Let me call an ambulance so we can get you checked out."

"No," I say quickly and shove myself to a sitting position. "No, I'm okay." Moving too quickly makes me dizzy again, but just a head rush. I'm fine. I didn't hit my head, and I might have a couple bruises, but I was lucky.

Lucky because Keenan pulled me out of the way. "What are you doing here?"

"Me?" The look on his face is a mixture of terror and

fury. "What are you doing walking out into traffic? You could have been killed?"

His arms are around me in a second, and everything about him from his stance to his voice speaks of protection. Fingers dig into my spine, and when I look up at him to meet his gaze, I see that same passion, and now possession. I feel it too, greedy for his touch.

I'm shaking, and for just a moment, I let myself lean into him. Keenan gather's me close, and that scent that seemed suffocating just a couple of minutes ago now seems comforting. I rest my forehead on his chest, and slowly his hand glides up my back to cradle my neck.

My heart is pounding and yet I feel exhausted, the adrenaline draining out of my system with the realization of safety. Keenan came after me. "You came after me," I say, voice muffled in his shirt.

"I couldn't let you walk away," he says softly. "And I'm glad I didn't. A few second later and…I don't want to think about that."

He doesn't have to fill in the blanks. My mind is already doing it for me more than adequately. "Thank you."

"And I might add," he says, with a smile I can hear, "we're in public. Broad daylight. Touching. And the world didn't come crashing down."

I pull away slowly. I don't want to, and running away from it clearly isn't working. Anxiety bubbles in my gut. I know that I'm playing with fire, but I also know that if I don't do something, this *will* turn into a regret.

Part of me wants to make it easy. Drag him back inside to that fancy office of his and let him fuck me ten ways till Sunday. Or I can be brave and hope that I know what the fuck I'm doing.

I clear my throat and straighten out my clothes as I look

at him. "I'll agree to dinner," I say, holding out a hand to stop him from interrupting. I can already see that he was going to. "But I have conditions."

The smile on Keenan's face is blinding. "Go ahead."

"No wearing a suit. Casual clothes only," I tell him.

He chuckles. "Okay."

"I pick the restaurant."

"Again, fine," he says.

Pulling my shoulders back, I meet his gaze square on. "And I pay."

Raised eyebrows. "Really?"

"It's that or nothing," I tell him. "We do this on my terms, or we make a clean break and never see each other again. Not even for a flower delivery."

"Cactus delivery, technically."

I roll my eyes. "You know what I mean."

"I'll do it," he says. "You let me know when and where."

Pulling my phone out of my pocket, I hand to him. Without a word, he takes it and puts in his number, but he's grinning like a fool and can't stop. "Are you sure you're okay? Do you need a car to get home?"

"I'm fine, I say. My car is a couple blocks away."

He looks me up and down one more time, as if reassuring himself that I was actually whole and healthy. "Then I'll see you tonight," he says with a wink before heading back inside.

I wait until he's completely out of sight before I let myself smile even a little.

8

KEENAN

I collapse onto the couch when I walk into my apartment earlier than I have in months. Even though today was a relatively light day work wise, I'm still exhausted. The amazing sex and the adrenaline of seeing Justine almost run over have taken it out of me.

But I wouldn't miss tonight's date for the world.

I'm happy that she's agreed to see me again—that I somehow convinced her that I wasn't this evil thing that she seems to think I am. It only took saving her life.

I can't shake the feeling of terror that I've had ever since I saw that car. If I'd been even three more steps away, I wouldn't have been able to save her. It's a sobering thought, and one that's been lodged in my gut all day.

She needs to be safe—I need to keep her safe. My instincts are screaming it. But there's nothing I can do about it. I just met her yesterday, and even though every cell is screaming that she's precious and needs to be protected, Justine would punch me for trying to control anything she did.

And I wouldn't blame her for that.

However, I'm used to being in control. I've curated the environment around me so that there's nothing that can't be predicted. And I think that's one of the reasons I'm so draw to her, aside from *everything*. She's wild. She can't be controlled. I love that. And at the same time it makes me anxious.

My phone buzzes in my pocket, and I manage to rally myself enough to check it. It's a text from Justine, and suddenly I'm feeling far more awake.

Eight o'clock. Lena's.

She adds the address as well.

I haven't heard of it. Is it any good?

I watch the little bubbles on the screen and imagine her in apartment typing. Is she in bed? My mental image of her is tousled and gorgeous, lounging on her bed while she texts me.

Honestly, it's delicious. I promise.

Anything else you can promise me?

A hesitation. *What do you mean?*

I laugh softly as I type. *I mean you're buying me dinner. Do you promise not to violate my honor? Just cause you're paying doesn't mean I'll owe you.*

Your honor is safe with me. You'll have to discard your honor on purpose.

That is tempting. Does this place have good desserts?

Delicious, why?

I can't keep the smirk off my face or the way my dick hardens in my pants. *You taste like strawberries,* I type out. *I thought maybe I'd just eat you.*

There's a long pause where there's no typing on her end. Long enough for me to wonder if I killed her entirely. But then, finally, two little words that make me stiffen to the point of pain, and blow out a breath in sudden arousal.

We'll see.

In that case, I can't wait. There's not too long before I need to leave. Though I haven't eaten there, I know where the restaurant is. It's close enough to walk from here. And since I'm going to wear casual clothes anyway, I might as well.

I take a quick shower, resisting the urge to just spend twenty minutes jacking off to the thought of tasting her again. Especially since the real thing is a possibility. Over the years I've gotten really good with my hand, but nothing compares to the real thing. Especially the electric intensity of our connection.

Jeans and a t-shirt are all I wear, per Justine's instructions. To be perfectly honest, I can't remember the last time I wore jeans out of the house. Sure, I dress casually at home, but whenever I leave home it's work related. And that means suits.

It's kind of nice to be out and about like this. It also reduces the risk of me being recognized. I'm not one of those wealthy people whose face is plastered everywhere so that they're famous for being rich. But I'm well known enough—especially in Portland—that it does happen from time to time.

When I see the tiny hole-in-the-wall restaurant, I know why she chose it. It's small, something that she thinks wouldn't be on my radar. But she's wrong. I love small and out of the way places. The reason I've never been to this place is that it's vegan food.

I don't hate it, and I've had some amazing vegan dishes, but I don't regularly seek it out.

And there, standing on the sidewalk, is Justine. Her hair is down again, and she's wearing a flowing dress that billows around her feet in the evening breeze. The light from the setting sun makes her glow, and I have the urge to capture this moment in my mind so that I'll never forget it.

Just then, she looks over at me. And it feels like a miracle when she smiles. Not a full one, but a small one. It's a smile of private joy and secrets. Of inside jokes and pretending. Something that I already wanted more of with her.

"Hi," she says as I walk up to her.

"Hello. Is this casual enough for you?" I take my time looking at her, enjoying the view of the gorgeous green dress that sets off her skin and eyes.

She smirks, a look that I could get used to. "I told you to be casual. I, however, never get to dress up at all. Besides, this isn't even that fancy."

"You look beautiful."

I nearly miss the subtle blush on her cheeks, but it's there for a moment. "Thank you."

"So Lena's?"

"It's really good, and it seemed like it's not something you would usually do. Very grungy. Not well known."

I grin at her. "Again with all the assumptions. You're right about one thing, I haven't been here. But unlike what you seem to think, I'm very open to new experiences."

Justine twists her lips to keep from smiling. "Fair enough. Let's see how you do."

She leads me inside the restaurant, and already I love the atmosphere. There are low hanging lights and living plants growing from moss farms in the walls. It feels a little like walking into a tropical paradise, and it feels even more that way when we exit onto a back patio with quaint tables and alcoves enclosed with sheer netting. We settle in one of those and wait for a server to come take our order.

I can already see another reason she wanted to come here when I look at the menu. The food is almost criminally inexpensive. Doing the math in my head, I almost can't imagine how this place breaks even.

"Before you ask how they stay open," she says, "the owner is independently wealthy and wanted to create a space that provides low cost, healthy food for the community. But it's so popular that they break even a good portion of the time."

I raise my eyebrows. "That's really impressive."

"Yeah, it is."

"Are you vegan?"

She shakes her head. "No. Vegetarian. But this place is one of my favorite places to eat. It's amazing, and you really can't beat the prices."

I look over the menu, and it does look amazing. When the waiter comes, Justine orders carrot and turmeric soup with roasted beans, and I order a ravioli pomodoro with cashews and tofu.

When our orders are taken, I notice her looking at me. "What?"

She blushes again. "Nothing, you just look nice out of the suit."

Primal satisfaction twists in my gut. I know I look good, but seeing the look in her eyes when she says it is an entirely different experience.

"You know what else is vegan?" she asks as the waiter brings back our food along with two shot glasses. "Vodka."

Justine takes hers and knocks it back, and I watch her swallow. Keep it together, Keenan. It's barely the beginning of dinner. You don't need to be sporting a boner the whole time. "I think I knew that," I say. "But it's always a little bit weird to think about."

The alcohol burns down my throat. Vodka isn't my usual go-to, but I'll take it. Anything to loosen us both up from the tension that's between us. It's a comfortable tension, but there is something strong connecting us. A connection that seems inexplicable.

And just as Justine predicted, the food is absolutely amazing. "Wow."

"I know right? It's so good. I come here for lunch all the time."

"Good to know."

"Oh, you're going to start stalking me?" She laughs.

I laugh. "Maybe. The only reason I didn't look you up last night was because I forgot to ask your name."

Justine leans closer to me, and I'm not even sure that she realizes when she does it. "Well you know it now."

"Yes," I say. "I know that you're Justine. You work at a non-profit that helps the elderly. Your best friend is an excellent florist." I lean close to whisper in her ear. "And your pussy tastes and feels like heaven.

She's frozen in a blush when I pull away. It's not a lie. Not even close to one. And that thing between us grows stronger. But as much as I would like to, I can't take her on the table in the middle of the restaurant.

Justine lifts her hand, and the waiter appears with two more vodka shots. She throws it back. "And other than the fact that you're richer than god, hot, and own a business, I know nothing about you."

"I'm normal. Just like you. I work too much, enjoy a good glass of whiskey at the end of the day." There's more to me of course, but I need to win her over further before she'll accept that I'm more than a stereotype. So instead I turn the questions back on her. Her favorite color is blue, she's a morning person, and her last name is Jackson.

Over the course of the conversation, we move closer and closer together, and by the time we're both finished with our plates, our legs are touching and we're practically sharing breath.

She calls the waiter over and pays the bill, and as she's handing it back, I catch her hand. "I'm not ready for this to be over yet."

"Is this the part where I ravish you in spite of your honor?" she asks.

"If you decided to ravish me, Justine, that would *be* the honor."

She lets me hold her hand as we leave, and I guide her down the street in the direction of my apartment. The river is nearby, and we cross to walk near it along the water. The sunset streaked sky is reflecting off the water, the evening cool and perfect. If there was a day for a perfect first date, this is it.

"So do you still think you know who I am?"

She's quiet as we walk, and I wait. It's a thoughtful silence. "I'm definitely less sure now. But I'm not sure I'll ever know for real, unless you tell me. If you're really different, then prove it."

I stop walking and press her back against the railing along the river. The sun is fading into nothing, and the sky is a smooth expanse of darkening blue. I miss the little pinpricks that would be visible by now if we weren't in the city. "Are you used to seeing stars? Or no?"

"I've lived here my whole life," she says. "So I'm used to them not being there. They are beautiful though, when you can see them."

I nod. "I've been here for a long time, but I don't think I'll ever be used to so few stars."

For a moment she looks confused, but that passes as both of us realize together that our bodies are pressed together and that current is binding us closer. With a sudden grin I lean closer. "We didn't have dessert," I say softly.

Her eyes widen. "I kind of forgot about it."

"I didn't," I say, gathering the fabric of her skirt into my hand as I look up and down the street. There's no one nearby, most people downtown are still in restaurants or bars or hanging out at more popular spots around the river. "There's one dessert I'm very interested in."

She grabs my arm, gasping as I slip my hand under her skirt and between her legs. There's nothing but pure heat in her eyes. "Am I violating your honor, Justine?"

"Please do." She bites her lips and relaxes into me more.

I'm harder than a rock in a second, because the fabric of her tiny panties are soaked, and she moans when I stroke my finger across her clit. From a distance, anyone looking at us would see just a couple close together. They wouldn't notice the way Justine's fingers are digging into my arms in desperation, or the way her lips part and cheeks flush with arousal.

I slip past the fabric of her panties with a groan. "You're soaking wet."

"I can't help it," she says. "It seems to be my default state around you."

"Just thinking about you makes me hard, Justine. I'm desperate for you. I can't explain it." I move my finger deeper, seeking her entrance and watching her chest rise and fall faster with excitement.

Justine shakes her head. "I shouldn't want you."

"Are you admitting that you do?" I ask with a smirk.

She groans as I slip inside her. "I think my pussy did that for me."

"Yes, it did."

I close the gap between us, letting my mouth fall on

hers, and we fall into each other again. The same way that we did earlier today. It feels dangerous and inevitable. And we need to get out of here before I bend her over the railing.

"My apartment is close," I whisper against her lips.

"Is it the penthouse?"

I laugh. "Yes it is."

She laughs too, but it's breathy and low. "I fucking knew it."

I help her rearrange her dress before pulling her down the sidewalk with me. We have to get there, and she feels the same. I don't even say hello to the doorman on the way in because we're moving so quickly. Scanning my card in the elevator, the doors aren't even closed before my lips are on hers again. When I scan my keycard, the elevator makes no stops, so I'm pulling the dress off her shoulders even before the doors open again.

The polite part of me thinks I should give her a tour of the place. But the feral part of me knows that we don't have that kind of time. Her dress hits the floor in the lobby along with her purse and shoes. I pull away long enough to take in the matching bra and panties she's wearing—all black lace against her creamy skin. Oh, fuck.

I scoop her into my arms and stride down the hallway to my bedroom. The room is dim with the last remaining light glowing in the windows, and I lay her out on the bed so she's spread before me like a feast. "I wasn't joking," I said. "You are my dessert."

Hooking my fingers into the elastic of her panties, I draw them down her legs and toss them aside. Then I'm pushing her legs apart and taking my fill. Justine moans as I lick into her, already shaking.

She tastes rich and sweet. Perfect.

I push her thighs wider so she's spread open, and I see

her grasp the comforter in tight fists. Her pussy is gorgeous, that perfect pink that matches her nipples, glistening in the fading light. I seal my mouth over her clit, sucking deep as I tease her from underneath, listening to the shake in her breath and feeling the growing tension in her legs.

"Tell me what you like," I say, whispering the words into her skin. There's nothing that I want more than to make her moan my name. I swirl my tongue over her clit before diving down and dipping into her entrance. Justine arches underneath me. "Tell me."

"I can't think," she says, more breath than words.

I crawl up her body until we're face to face and kiss her hard, letting her taste herself on my tongue. The way I'm laying now, my cock is pressed up against her spread legs. So close, and so far.

"Do you want me to suck your clit until you scream?"

"Yes."

I move my mouth to her neck and shoulder, pushing the strap of her bra off with my teeth. "Do you want me to fuck you with my tongue?"

"Fuck," she mutters as I sink down her body again.

"I can tease you until you're begging me," I say, peppering the skin around her belly button with soft kisses. "And then tell you no."

"You wouldn't dare," she says, looking down at me.

"Wouldn't I? We could find out."

She smirks down at me. "You still think you can boss me around?"

"I think I can make you feel good enough that you won't care who's calling the shots. You'll just want to come."

I graze my teeth against her inner thigh, thoroughly enjoying the shudder that passes through her. I know exactly what to do now. And I take my time. I slowly lick her thighs and move closer, pressing kisses and licks to the creases of her legs. On her mound. Everywhere but where she wants me to be. Completely random so she never knows where I'm going to touch her next. I love it. She doesn't.

"Fuck, you're going to kill me," she says.

"We can't have that," I mutter, barely brushing my lips across her clit.

"*Oh*," she makes the sound before biting her lip, not wanting to show me how much she wants it. Even now we're in that battle—the one that makes me want to push her buttons more. Further. The one that drives the spark between us.

I go back to teasing before I lick her once. So softly, but her legs contract at the feeling and I push them wide again. Slowly I build up the way I'm touching her. Kissing and licking and sucking every part of her, harder and harder until I cover her in one long stroke of my tongue, and she breaks, shaking and groaning, more of that pure flavor flooding my mouth.

Once isn't enough. Not nearly. I plunge my tongue deep inside her, fucking her as the orgasm runs through and straight into another one. Justine cries out, her voice echoing off my walls, arching into my tongue.

Fuck, I'll never have enough. I need more. Right now.

I strip off my clothes and grab a condom before rejoining her on the bed. She's still lost in the aftermath of her orgasm, and already reaching for me. I pull her in to a kiss before turning her over and slamming into her from behind.

Perfect heat and epic pleasure. It's just as explosive as the first time we came together. I can't breathe. Just moving on instinct, I drive in to the hilt over and over. I can't hold myself back, and I don't try to.

"Fuck, yes," Justine cries out, and I let myself go.

I fuck with a frenzy, letting lighting build in my spine until it breaks, the release completely blinding me. My own voice echoes as I finish, and we collapse together, breathless and spent.

She laughs softly, turning toward me as I slip away to dispose of the condom before coming back. "That was a pretty good dessert."

"Better than the ones at Lena's?"

"I don't know about that, but easily just *as* good."

She's smirking and I drag her to me so I can kiss her. "I guess I'll just have to work harder next time."

"Maybe," she says, resting her head on my chest. "But before that, I might need some actual dessert."

9

JUSTINE

The faint chime wakes me with a start. My phone. Chiming from where I left it. Where did I leave it? I focus. I'm not in my bed. Where the hell am I?

The sun is just rising through the windows and I look over to the handsome, peaceful, sleeping face of Keenan. I'm in Keenan's bed.

He looks even more perfect in sleep, totally relaxed and unaware of his own beauty. I hadn't intended to stay all night. But he fed me chocolate for dessert and then we had more amazing sex. Slower the next time, but no less passionate.

The chemistry between us is indescribable. It sings like a living thing between us. Why did I wake up? Oh right. My phone. Where I left it in my purse which is on the floor along with the rest of my clothes.

Slowly, I creep out of the bed. It's a little chilly, but nothing unbearable. I find my purse and dress and shoes scattered across the foyer. It's a total cliché. I grab everything and bring it back to the bedroom before creeping under the covers again. It's five a.m. I have to wake up soon anyway for an early client, but I'm tired enough that I want to hit snooze a little bit.

The text is from Lila. I told her that I was going on a date last night, and there are a bunch of texts from her asking where I am and if I'm okay. The last one is the one that woke me.

Got up to use the bathroom and saw you still hadn't texted. Please just let me know that you're not dead in a ditch somewhere.

I smile and text her back. *Hey, sorry. Very much not dead. It was a good date.* I pause and look over at Keenan. *A very good date.*

That's a fucking understatement.

I don't expect her to answer right now, not when it's this early. For a few minutes I let myself rest with my eyes closed until the sunrise outside is bright enough that I can't ignore it and I need to make sure that I have enough time to get home and change before I go and visit Harold. My early bird client that prefers his visits to be absolutely first thing in the morning.

Last night I used Keenan's bathroom, and I know that it's huge, and has one of the most luxurious showers that I've ever seen. I don't think that he'll mind too much if I use it. At least I hope not.

The shower is clean white marble, spacious with those

heads that spray water from all angles. It's like being caught in a storm of water in absolutely the best way.

Keenan made a joke about this shower last night in the middle of him delivering yet another ridiculous orgasm. Fuck, he was good. We were good together. Even after all that, I want more of him, and I feel myself growing wet. I don't have time to wait for him to wake up, as much as I want to, but my hand creeps between my legs, seeking quick pleasure that won't be nearly as satisfying. I'm slick enough that it's easy, and it won't take long.

A hand snakes around my waist and I nearly scream before I realize that it's Keenan behind me. Every inch of his lean length, cock pressing against my ass. One arm locks across my chest, holding me to him while the other replaces mine. "If you wanted more," he says low in my ear, "I would have said yes."

"I know."

Keenan doesn't let me move away, instead he keeps me pinned to his body, and teasing me. His lips graze my neck, and he finds a rhythm with his fingers that makes me tense. Pleasure rises, sure and sweet and fast. He's relentless, using everything he learned about my body to drag the orgasm from me.

It's not explosive. It rolls in like the tide. Smooth and inevitable, covering my whole body with bliss before fading away and leaving me gasping under the stream.

Keenan doesn't stop there, helping me wash, running soap over my body before lathering my hair. There are few things in life that rival one's hair being washed. It gives me chills. I could live for this kind of luxury, and I immediately stop the thought in its tracks.

Even though this has been amazing, Keenan and I are

still from two different worlds, and still stand for very different things.

Keenan hands me a towel when we step out of the shower and pulls me in for a kiss when I wrap myself in it. It's comfortingly domestic. Not necessarily in a bad way. "I'm sorry I didn't wake you up," I tell him. "Believe me, I would love nothing more than to play hooky with you. Stay in bed and have sex all day. But I have an early client."

He smiles at me. This isn't a smirk or anything meant to rile me up. It's just a smile. "It's okay. I know that I'll see you soon."

Yesterday I might have been upset by that assumption. But now it feels right. I will see him again. The thing between us is too real to be denied. "Thanks, though I'm sorry I can't stay and...help." I glance down at his erection.

Keenan chuckles. "I'll survive, don't worry, but I might step back into the shower."

I bite my lip. "Okay."

"I'll text you later," he says, stepping back into the spray.

I watch him for a moment, and he looks at me as his hand starts to move, and I blow him a kiss before leaving. I need to leave before I drop the damn towel and call in sick. I quickly dress. I'm going to need to move fast to get back to my car and apartment and change, but I do make it.

I'm right on time pulling up to our offices. Sometimes I do the actual grocery shopping, but for the most part—especially for clients like Harold who are early in the morning—the shopping is taken care of by someone else and I just pick up the groceries before heading over.

But when I walk inside, it's not the normal happy atmosphere that I'm used to experiencing in the morning. Everyone looks a little somber.

"What's going on?"

Morgan, my supervisor, looks at me. "We got word that 120 Asher is going to be demolished in two weeks."

That's Harold's building. "What?"

"Yeah, we had no idea. The permits came through yesterday I guess, and some developer is going ahead with a project that will get rid of the building and the park behind it. I guess the residents are going to be compensated."

"Holy shit." Dread pools in my stomach. The building where Harold lives is pretty old, and it houses more than a few clients. Compensation for being displaced is great, but a lot of these people have owned their apartments for many years. The check they're likely to get probably won't cover the absurd cost of a new place to live or a nursing home.

The park behind the house provides much needed exercise and fresh air for a lot of people living in that building. Yeah, the building is a little run down, but it's not something that needs to be demolished.

"Yeah," Morgan says. "We're going to see what we can do but it came out of nowhere. You were already planning to help us with the downtown demonstration, right?"

"Yeah, of course."

That one was the one that I had mentioned to Rose. Gathering signatures from people to make sure some downtown green space was preserved and not sold off to make more high-rise buildings.

"Well that's been pushed aside for this," she says. "This is way more urgent."

I nod. "I'll do whatever you need me to."

"For now, just see your clients. I've got to try to get hold of people on the city council. And after that we'll see what we can do about organizing. And if the worst of it does happen, we're going to need people to help find new placements."

Fuck. This really is bad. If developers are going after older buildings, it's only a matter of time before all of our clients are hit. I can see someone easily trying to justify demolishing Rose's building. I can think of a bunch of them that could be targeted for this.

I grab the first of Harold's groceries and start to move them out to my car. This is ridiculous. What kind of asshole would want to displace a bunch of people? Especially seniors with nowhere else to go?

My stomach curls in fear. "Morgan, which company is doing the demolishing?" Please don't be him. Please be literally anybody but him. If there's any good in this universe, it will give me this small favor.

"Silverman & Blake," she says.

The bag slips from my hands and crashes to the floor, spilling cans of soup that go rolling. "Shit," I say, scrambling to pick them up before they go everywhere.

Morgan is by my side in a second. "Are you okay?"

"Yeah," I say. "It just slipped."

But that's a lie. I'm very much not okay. Not after hearing that. Not after knowing that I slept with someone who could be this callous. Not just slept with him, but let him in. Thought about the possibility of continuing on a path with him.

My heart and body both still want that, and the news that he could do this makes me ache. Maybe it was a mistake. Maybe he doesn't know who lives there.

Or maybe he does, and he's exactly who I thought he was all along.

What do I do now?

10

KEENAN

Today has been a fucking amazing day. From waking up with Justine to that moment in the shower and how hard I came after, to the seeming wave of sunshine that I've been riding ever since. Everything seems a little bit brighter and easier.

I sent Justine a text just before noon asking her if she once again wanted to have dinner. No response yet, but I have high hopes. Especially after that smile that she gave me this morning.

Justine isn't like anyone that I've ever met, and deep down I know that it's more than just a simple attraction. There's something between us, and now that we've connected, I'm determined to see it through one way or another.

I check the time. I suppose it's okay to text her again. It's been a couple of hours.

Hey. I've been thinking of you.

. . .

She's probably working, so I don't worry when she doesn't respond right away. I just start to lose myself in my work again. We're planning a new expansive development to the north, and it's really exciting. Open land provides far more ground-up possibilities than the lots in the city usually provide. So we're designing an all-inclusive community. Everything from student living for the local college to restaurants and a coworking space alongside the housing.

It's honestly the most excited that I've been about a project in a long time. Doing this, it can be a little boring sometimes. The same forms and papers and steps and approvals over and over again. It can be monotonous, even if the end product is usually rewarding.

I lose myself in my work so thoroughly that the next time I look up it's the end of the workday, and there's still been no response from Justine. Anxiety suddenly bubbles in my gut. After the close call of the accident yesterday, that's where my thoughts go. Is she all right?

I type out another text to her. Miraculously, because of my mood, I've gotten through all the work I absolutely have to do today. And if she wanted to join me out or at home, that would be wonderful.

I'm heading home. I'd love to see you, if you're free.

I walk the short distance home—as I do most days. Justine would probably laugh and tell me that she would expect me to be driving some absurd luxury car. And I have the cars. Several of them. But Portland is a beautiful city, and especially in the summer I prefer to walk.

No text from Justine when I get home, and none while

I'm eating later or during the time I decide to read. It's so rare that I have the time, it's good to stretch out and relax my mind in that way. I really should do it more often.

When I'm about to go to bed, I send one final text saying good night, but at this point I don't expect any kind of response. It's not exactly a surprise that my mind doesn't allow me to fall asleep. Because I can't stop thinking about her and wondering if she's okay.

And if she is okay, then why hasn't she answered? Everything was fine when she left this morning. More than fine. She seemed excited at the prospect of seeing me again, and reluctant to leave at all. What possibly could have changed?

I don't like problems that I can't solve, and it's not something that I can solve if I don't have the reason behind it. Maybe she just had a long day. Maybe her phone died. Maybe I'll wake up to more texts from her.

Either way, there's no chance that I'm sleeping right now. I get up and make my way up to the roof. No matter what anyone says, owning a penthouse comes with its benefits. Roof access is one of those.

I've remodeled the roof into a patio garden. Comfortable chairs and chaise lounges along with flowering plant boxes and displays. I think it's a place that Justine would like if she saw it, and I'm hoping that I get to show it to her at some point.

Settling into one of my favorite chairs, I look at the sky. There's a shocking lack of stars here thanks to the city's glow. I do love this city, and the view from this building is undeniably spectacular, but I'm partial to a view of the open sky, even if it is mostly devoid of stars.

Looking up always reminds me of my favorite place in the world. A field filled with fireflies, a little to the south. Close enough to the coast that you could smell the ocean.

And if you really put your mind to it, you could hear the sea. Or maybe it was my imagination like seashells. Either way, I liked to imagine.

The sky looked so big. Infinite. The stars bright enough to touch, the complete absence of artificial light making it possible to see the Milky Way.

I'll never forget those nights. I spent a lot of them in that field, staring at the stars until my eyes burned with exhaustion, choking on humidity and heat, trying to block out the lonely thoughts. But as lonely as it always was...

It was quiet. Peaceful.

There was no fighting, screaming, or yelling.

I haven't been there in years, and in the time since this roof has become that peaceful place for me. But I don't feel particularly peaceful tonight. I feel anxious, and the mood that I was riding all day is fading. Getting up, I head back inside. I don't want to cloud the space with my racing thoughts, so instead I head back inside and say a small prayer that I can get some sleep.

11

JUSTINE

"You fucked him, didn't you," Rose says with a grin when she opens the door. She takes one look at me, up and down, and cracks into a giant grin.

"I'll never understand how you manage to do that," I say, stepping around her into her apartment. Rose wants to make a cake for her friend's birthday, so for the first time ever, she actually called me and asked me to drop off some special ingredients for said cake, which I'm happy to do.

But I should have known that it would have turned into this.

"Uh oh," she says. "That doesn't sound good. Don't tell me you actually regret it."

Placing the bag of ingredients on the counter, I sigh. "Yes and no."

"Do I need to make tea?"

I glance at my phone. I've got plenty of time, and Rose is kind of the one that got me into this mess in the first place, so I could use her advice. "Yeah, I think so."

"Sit down and tell me what happened."

I do. I leave out the gory details of all the sex, but I give her a decent idea of what happened and exactly how mind-blowing it was. Followed by the revelation two days ago that he's about to destroy the homes of a bunch of people just like her.

Keenan has been texting me, but I haven't responded. I have no idea what I would even say. I'm furious and sad, and most of all, I wish that things were different. But they're not. It's not like I didn't know something like this was a possibility. I was just hoping that it wouldn't happen.

When I've finished utterly spilling my guts, the water is boiling and Rose is pouring the tea.

"But the sex was good?"

I laugh in spite of myself. "Yes, it was very good. Amazing, actually."

"Well I'm glad you don't regret that part of it."

I shrug as she hands me the cup. "It doesn't solve everything else."

"Neither does running away," Rose says.

I make a face. "How did I know that you were going to say that?"

"Because," she sits down across from me, "that's the secret to really good advice. It's only ten percent telling someone something they don't know, and ninety percent confirming the thing they already knew but don't want to face."

"God, I hate it when you're right," I mutter.

"You actually love it."

I laugh into my cup. "But in all seriousness, Rose, what do I do? I can't be someone who supports that kind of...monstrosity."

"Have you talked to him about it? He's at the very top of

the chain. You're on the ground with the people. It's entirely possible he doesn't know who lives in the building or what the demolition will do. And continuing to avoid him will only make you more anxious about it."

I grit my teeth. She has a point, but at the same time I'm dreading that conversation. Because what if he *does* know? What if he fooled me into thinking that he was different and was exactly what I thought?

But Rose is once again right. Drawing it out to an impossible length will only make it harder. It if needs to end, better to have it over with quickly than worry about it, avoid it, and having to move on anyway.

"You're right, of course, but it doesn't make it easier."

"Of course not, but life rarely is easy. And sometimes the harder the thing, the better the reward."

My mood is all over the place when I leave Rose's apartment. I feel lighter, but when I look at my phone and see a text from Lila asking if I've heard from the *very good date* again, or if I'm ghosting him, my mood plummets again. She asked me yesterday for more details and I was too sad to give her anyway, even though I would normally spill everything to my best friend.

Another text comes a few minutes later, this time asking if *he's* ghosting *me*. I almost wish that were the case. I would expect that. I gave him what he wanted and then he could disappear. But no, he keeps messaging me. Telling me good morning and good night and occasionally that he's thinking of me.

Every time I see one of his messages, my fingers twitch with the urge to message him back. I don't answer Lila's questions, instead telling her that I'll talk to her later about everything. I'm heading to the office to get petition sheets to save the building. Morgan organized things quickly. It seems like there might be some wiggle room on the city council, and if we can gather enough signatures to prove that there's a vested community interest, we can stop the project.

Or at least I hope that we can.

It's hot today, and I'm already sweating, but it's working to my advantage. People want to sign as quickly as possible so they can get to wherever they're going. I'm getting a good number of signatures, which is nice. Canvassing can be a thankless job. People avoid making eye contact with you or cross the street so that they don't have to talk to you. But since this is a quieter and more residential neighborhood, people have been a little friendlier and willing to sign to save a historic building and park.

"Justine."

My stomach drops, and my heart rate spikes as I turn to find Keenan on the sidewalk behind me. I know that I need to talk to him, but now is not the time or place, especially when I'm trying to figuratively cock block him.

"I'm working, Keenan. Now isn't the time."

He swallows. "That's fair, but before I go, can you tell me why you've been avoiding me? I just want to know so that I can fix it."

I square my jaw and gather my courage. "To get where you are I'm sure you're very smart, Keenan. And you know enough about me now. You could figure it out. If you tried."

Reaching out, he takes the clipboard out of my hand and scans the top pages that explain who we are and what we're trying to save. He then flips to the pages beyond it and looks at all the signatures that I've collected so far. The expression on his face is somber.

"Can I borrow your pen?" he asks.

"Why?"

Keenan just holds out his hand, and I give him the pen. And I think my jaw nearly hits the sidewalk when he signs his name under all the others listed.

"What are you doing?"

He sighs, handing pen and clipboard back to me. "I get it now. Why you haven't been speaking to me."

"But why would you sign it? Are you making fun of me?"

He closes his eyes for a moment. "You always think I'm doing that. I'm not."

"But this is *you*, Keenan. Silverman & Blake. Your company is in charge of this teardown."

He nods. "I know. That's why I'll stop it."

"What?" I feel like words aren't computing in my brain right now.

And then he shrugs. Keenan *shrugs*. "I can put this project someplace else. It won't be ideal, but I can figure it out once I talk to my partner and some other people. I can fix it. I promise."

My vision turns red, and suddenly rage that I didn't realize I was holding comes flying out. "Are you fucking kidding me?" I throw the pen at him, but it doesn't feel like enough, so I throw the clipboard too. The papers come loose and scatter all over the sidewalk. He looks shocked, and I don't even care.

"You can *fix* it? You're the one that broke it in the first place! The fact that it's just as easy as that is disgusting, Keenan. Tear down buildings just to build more without a thought just because it suits whatever whim you've got in your head without any thoughts about the consequences for the real people who live in these places. And because you want to fuck me you'll bend over backwards to save this one?

"Do you understand how fucking furious that makes

me? These are people's *lives,* but it's nothing but a bottom line to you. Everything is about money and profit and nothing else."

I start to gather the papers from the ground before a breeze starts up and takes them away. I'm still going to need all of these signatures. Without a word, Keenan bends down to help me gather all the rest of the stuff, including the pen and clipboard.

"You're right," he says.

For the second time in our conversation my jaw feels like it's hitting the ground. "What?"

"There's definitely a power imbalance," he says. "Between you and me. Between me and almost everyone. But I've never met anyone that would tell me something like this to my face. They're all too afraid of me, or too after the money you mentioned. Nobody bothered to suggest that it might be a mistake. Or that it was the incorrect path. There were never any questions.

"I knew there would be some displacement, but I wasn't told that it would be elderly citizens who are vulnerable. If you think that I would intentionally destroy lives like that, you must really think that I'm a monster."

I swallow, sitting on the sidewalk. My knees are shaking enough from the adrenaline that I'm not sure that they would support me. "I've met other CEOs, Keenan. They've never cared. And when I heard it was you…"

He laughs softly, without humor. "I'm not saying that it doesn't make sense. But I can only do so much. I can't make up for the actions of other people, but I can try to make sure that mine are solid and okay. This place was literally numbers on paper for me. I've never been here or to the park."

My stomach unclenches and my nausea eases. Rose was right. As fucking always. The woman is psychic. I really swear that she is. She said she thought as much. "I'm sorry," I say. "For not talking to you about it first." I'm not sure I can apologize entirely for everything I said. Keenan still has a lot to prove.

He hands me the papers that he's gathered from the sidewalk and helps me to my feet. My soul feels so much calmer than it did, even though I exploded. "If you're serious," I say, "about cancelling the project and not tearing all of this up to create more condos for glitzy tech bachelors, then I'll think about letting you take me on a second date…if you still want to."

"Oh, I want to," he says.

"After all, you do owe me a meal. I paid for the last one." He takes a step closer to me, and I let him. I know why he's hesitating. I gave him good reason. "I'm sorry," I say again.

When he wraps his arm around my waist and kisses me gently, I know that I'm forgiven. At least partly. "I'm not like them," he says softly. "I promise."

Placing my hand to his chest, I breathe in his scent that I've somehow already missed even though it's only been two days. "I know."

He smiles, lips against my forehead. "I will give you reason to trust me, Justine."

"How did you know that I was here?"

Keenan actually laughs now. "I asked Lila if she knew a way to contact you, and she figured out that I was the 'one you had gone on a date with,' in her words. So she told me where you were and I came. I'm glad she told me, so I could see it. The park, the people, you."

"I'll give her hell for it later," I promise. "Though it's

probably going to be her giving me hell. Since I decided to fuck her most important client."

He grins. "I'm her most important client?"

"Shut up."

"Will do," he says, and kisses me again.

12

JUSTINE

I'm in trouble.

As usual.

Keenan talked me into a second date, and this time, it's on his terms. I let him into my world. Cheap delicious food and casual atmosphere, and this time he told me that he wants to let me into his world. To show me that money isn't always evil. And part of that is dressing up.

The only problem is, the only remotely fancy dress I had was the one I wore on our first date. I wasn't lying when I said it wasn't that fancy, but it's the only thing I have. So now I'm standing in front of Lila's closet. Lamenting.

"You really don't have to do this," I say.

Her smile is literally a mile wide. "Oh, I really, really do."

"It's not weird for you?"

Lila smirks. "What, that I sent you on an errand and you ended up with a date that absolutely rocked your world and who also happens to be my best client? Nah. I think it's great."

I sit down on her bed. "I think I'm going to throw up."

"You are *not*. Now get up, you have to try some stuff on."

She starts pulling out dresses that are fancier than anything that I've ever seen her wear.

"Why do you have these?"

"Never know when you'll need them," she says, laughing. "No, you know my mom. She's always trying to get me to be better than a florist and sending me clothes to match what she thinks my status ought to be. I've only kept a few that I actually liked."

"Well, thanks." They're definitely better than anything I own.

"I really want you to knock his socks off."

I run my fingers over a deep purple dress with a short skirt. "You seem to be pretty invested in this."

Lila turns and looks at me. "J, you've been single for years. You work yourself to the bone helping everyone, including me. This is the most interest you've shown in anyone, even if y'all are some kind of star-crossed lovers. I want you to be happy, and if he's going to make you happy, then I am one-hundred percent behind you."

I laugh. "Okay then."

She tosses a red number at me. "Put that on."

"I'm not totally sure that red is my color."

"Put it on." I do, and she makes a face. "Yeah, no good. I really think it's that one," she points to the purple one that I was looking at. "The color will be nice with your eyes."

The fabric shimmies down over my hips and flows around my thighs. The dress doesn't quite reach my knees, and I love the way it feels.

Lila looks me up and down. "Fuck yes."

"Really?"

"If I were into women, I would be all over you," she grins.

I step over to her mirror against the door and look at

myself. "Wow." My reflection doesn't look like me. I can't remember the last time I've worn something this...nice. I've never bothered with fancy clothes because I haven't needed them, and the people that I hang out with were the same as me.

I don't know what it says about me that I like the way this looks on me, but I do.

"Here," Lila says, putting a pair of silver high heels on the ground beside me. "Put these on."

When I slip into the shoes, I feel powerful. Like someone who could take on the world. Or in this case, a date with Keenan Silverman. "You're a magician, Lila."

She giggles. "I'm not a magician for putting you in clothes that actually fit and happen to cost more than ten dollars at the thrift store."

"Hey. That one pair of jeans cost twenty."

She fluffs my hair a little. "This is definitely the one. Do I need to do your hair and make-up too?"

"Hair, yes. Make-up, no."

"All right," Lila takes a deep breath. "Get the dress off. Time to fairy godmother this shit."

I sit down and let her start to curl my hair, and sigh. "Is this really a good idea? After everything?"

"Has he cancelled the project?"

"As far as I know, yes."

"Then sure," she says.

"But what happens when there's a project that he can't just move? At some point there's going to be a conflict that we can't solve."

"*Or* maybe knowing you will change the way that he thinks about taking projects in the first place," she says. "Maybe he'll make an effort to see the humans behind the numbers before actually agreeing to things."

He did tell me that he would give me reason to trust him, and I need to give him that chance.

"What made you this jumpy about stuff like this?" Lila asks.

"You know."

She shakes her head. "No, I don't. It's never come up."

Lila and I are best friends now, but in the grand scheme of things we haven't known each other that long. I thought she'd known. "In college I got really close with one of my clients. I was studying social work, and I got to know the whole family. They were living in a building and they were being displaced because of the same thing. The developer wanted to build new apartments. We got enough traction to stop the demolition. The building was fine, it just wasn't what the developer wanted."

I sigh and keep going. "But he went around us. He paid off the people that he needed to pay off in order to continue the demolition, and he decided that he didn't want to wait. The people were practically dragged out of their home so that the building could be torn down. They imploded it. Many of the people living there lost their possessions as well as their homes."

Lila makes a sound of disgust. "That's really fucked up."

"Tell me about it."

"But Keenan isn't like that."

"No," I say. "He's not."

I cross my heart inside that that's true.

Half an hour later I'm polished and primped, hair curling around my shoulders and waiting outside for Keenan to pick me up. I told him to collect me from Lila's house. It didn't seem that important to go all the way home.

There's no mistaking which car is his when it turns onto the street. A sleek sports car that practically oozes sex appeal the same way that he does. I'm not sure how a car manages to do that, but it does. And when Keenan gets out of the car, I swear that all the air in the world has disappeared.

He's wearing a silvery gray suit that is tailored exactly to his body. It hugs his shoulders and his hips and makes my mouth water with lust.

Keenan is looking at me the same way that I'm looking at him, and I'm tempted to suggest that we skip the date entirely. But he's walking toward me now, wrapping me in his arms and kissing me deeply. "You look stunning."

"So do you."

"Are you ready to let me wine and dine you?"

I smile. "Unless you want to move to dessert first."

"Tempting," Keenan says. "But fair is fair. I owe you a dinner."

He opens the door for me, and I slip into the car and deeper into his world.

* * *

My heels are hanging off the tips of my fingers as Keenan carries me off the elevator and into his apartment. I'm deliciously tipsy, and I can't remember a time where I've truly felt this relaxed and happy.

But with that happiness also comes confusion.

Keenan took me to a restaurant where the meal cost more than my monthly salary and the wine we had practically tasted like gold. Everything was delightful and pretty. There was elegant music and dancing, and we spun under a chandelier that glittered.

I may have had too much to drink, but everything

seemed so lovely that I couldn't help myself. It felt like I was living in a fairytale...and I liked it.

But none of that would have been possible without Keenan and the wealth that he has. It was eye opening to see that it wasn't all bad. Somewhere along the way I started to think that there was nothing good that could come of it. But he managed to sweep me away. Perfect conversation and dancing, and enough casual touches that I'm ready for him to take me to bed.

I'm more sober now than I was at the restaurant, but still buzzed enough to know that I want to fuck him senseless. But first, I have a plan.

"You know," I say to him, dropping the heels on the carpet on the way to his room. "We didn't have dessert."

Keenan chuckles. "Yes we did."

"Go with it," I whisper.

"Okay, what would you like for dessert then, Justine?"

Leaning up, I press my lips to his ear. "Your cock in my mouth."

I swear that he nearly drops me. "That's not what I was expecting you to say."

"That was the idea."

When we reach the bedroom, he lets me slip down to the floor onto my feet, but I keep going to my knees. I want him now. I want to taste him the way that he tasted me.

Undoing his belt, I find him already hard. His cock is just as gorgeous as the rest of him. Thick and long and straight. I could be more subtle, but not tonight. Wrapping my lips around his head, I suck him down. Keenan groans, his hands falling into my hair. He had almost as much to drink as I did, and he's just as aroused.

His skin tastes like smoke and salt as I swirl my tongue over him, teasing that spot just beneath his head. Further and further I push myself down, trying to take as much of him as I can. But I'm not even close. He's too long, and I can feel him at the edge of my throat.

"Jesus," he says.

I laugh, pulling back. "Nope, just Justine."

His laugh strangles into another groan as I sink back onto him, setting up a rhythm on his shaft. Sinking down deep and pulling back, again and again until he's gasping, using his hands to help me move faster, franticly fucking my mouth.

Focusing on just the head, I suck hard, and feel him start to shake. Just that tiny spot is enough. I can feel it, and I work him with shallow strokes. Glancing up, Keenan looks ragged. His lips are parted and eyes closed, completely lost in the pleasure that I'm giving him. I love the feeling of being responsible for that.

And when he spills himself across my tongue, I swallow all of it. It's mine.

Keenan curses under his breath, fingers tightening in my hair to hold me still as he finishes, bursts of his cum filling my mouth.

He pulls me off my knees and spins me around, stripping me out of my dress in seconds before discarding his own clothes. We fall onto the bed together, tangled, kissing, reaching with hands to explore every part that we can reach.

I open my eyes and startle at a sharp shape near me, and then I start to laugh. The cactus is sitting on his bedside table. "You kept it."

"Of course I did," he says. "You picked it out. And you're right, it's not going to die. A reminder that I need my ego poked once in a while."

His eyes are shining in the darkness, and the mood between us shifts from frantic to sensual. Every movement is slow and deliberate, and no less connected. I help him put on the condom and guide him into me. We start slow together, mouths sealed against each other.

This is a different kind of passion. One that's deep and trusting and totally open. Everything between us builds together. Breath and pleasure are totally synced, and when I fall apart in his arms, he's there with me. We fall into our own pleasure and then each other's, the orgasm just as deep and just as pure.

Keenan pulls me close after, wrapping us both in blankets, and I cannot remember a time that I've felt this safe. This seems so simple and easy. Something more than I could have imagined...

But even as I'm falling asleep, I don't dare say the words.

13

KEENAN

"You can't just cancel a project without notice, Keenan."

I sigh. "I'm not cancelling it, I'm deciding to move it. You were right when you asked before. We got pushback. I didn't realize the people that lived in the building were a vulnerable population."

Brandon is seething. I can see it as I stand in the doorway to his office. "And you were right when you said that the numbers lined up and that everyone would be compensated. The demolition is already on the books for Monday. I got them to move it up because the permits were ready and they were stellar. We are ready to roll."

I shake my head. "That doesn't even make sense. That barely gives anyone time in the building to find new living spaces."

"Like I said, they're being compensated handsomely." He practically rolls his eyes. "I'm sure that they don't own anything that's actually that valuable."

For the first time I'm seeing the truly ugly side of Brandon. Or maybe it was always there, and I didn't notice. Or chose not to. Justine crashing into my life has given me a new perspective, and it's a good one. I can't play god in people's lives, and I would never want to. "It's the right move to delay this project indefinitely," I say, "and that's the end of the discussion."

"Excuse me?"

I shrug. "This is the right call. I'm sorry that you don't see it that way, but it's the truth. I called to pull the permits an hour ago. You couldn't go ahead without my okay anyway."

"You're fucking pulling rank right now? Jesus, Keenan. What kind of stick do you have up your fucking ass?" Brandon yells, standing up from behind his desk. "This project is one of the most profitable ROIs we've ever had at the company, and you're going to throw it away over a few old people?"

I stare him down, putting ice in my glare. "This company is doing better than ever, and we have plenty of other projects to work on. Pick another one. Any one. And we'll revisit this project when it's appropriate."

Brandon shakes his head. "I heard you fucked one of those activist sluts, but I never thought that she'd actually get to you." He looks a little guilty when he sees my face, but he doesn't back down.

If I didn't need him to actually go along with what I'm saying, I would have a hard time not punching him in the face right now. As it is, I'm struggling to keep my hands in my pockets from folding into fists.

"Get your head out of your ass by Monday, Brandon."

I don't wait to hear his response. Whatever it is, I'm not interested.

* * *

The field looks exactly the same as I remember it. Justine agreed to come away with me for a weekend, and this is a stop on the way to the coast where I plan to keep her in bed the entire weekend. But this is a nice reminder, given that I was just thinking about this the other night.

"I used to come here all the time," I say. "I would lay in the middle of the field and just watch the stars and try to find new constellations that no one had ever found before."

"Really?" Justine says. "How did you get here?"

I take her hand and pull her further into the field. "I'll show you. In the evening this whole field is absolutely swarming with fireflies. Or at least it used to be. I haven't been down here in years."

We follow the path that I used to walk, to the tiny isolated house on the outskirts of one of the local farms. "This is it," I say.

"What is?"

I smile. "This is where I grew up."

Justine gazes at the small house in wonder. "You *lived* here? No wonder you asked if I missed the stars."

"This was my aunt's house," he says. "She worked on the nearby farm and she took me in for a while when my parents weren't able to care for me anymore. They were far more interested in their drugs and fighting each other for every cent of drug money than they were in being parents."

"Oh my god," she says, leaning on my arm. "I'm so sorry."

"Don't be," I say. "Coming here is probably the best thing that could have happened to me. I learned what it meant to be normal and healthy. What hard work meant, and that what I had always known wasn't the way the world had to be.

"Here, I figured out how to take control of my life. And I

became determined to make it so no one could take anything from me by force again. That's why I do what I do. The money was never about…making other people feel less. I just wanted to make sure that I never had to worry." I smile. "It worked better than I could have hoped."

Justine rises up on her toes and captures my mouth with hers. I kiss her back—a kiss of understanding and consolation.

"Thank you for showing me this," she says. "It's beautiful. I'm sorry about your aunt."

I laugh. "Oh she's not dead, she's just too old to do farm work. I bought her a place in the city so it was easier for me to visit. I should go more than I do, but half the time I go she's busier than I ever imagined she would be. I swear she's the life of the party."

"I think I would like her," she says.

"I'm pretty sure that you would. I actually pay for a similar service to the one you work for to help her with her groceries. She's still independent, and loves to do her own thing. But her eyes aren't good enough to drive anymore, and she likes the glamour of having someone deliver her groceries. She tells me that it makes her feel like a queen."

Justine laughs. "Which service? I probably know it. There aren't that many of us."

"Delovery," I say, and I watch her face transform into shock. "What?"

"That's where I work. What's your aunt's name?"

"Ellen Bassa."

"Oh my god." She's laughing now. "I've never met her, but I've heard stories. You're right, she really is the life of the party. I think that she would be best friends with my client Rose. They seem like they'd be two peas in a pod."

I smile and start to walk her back toward the car. "Maybe we can get them together."

"Rose would love that. One of her friends recently passed away and she could use some new ones."

We're quiet as we walk back through the field, and I feel more at peace than I have in a long time. Being here with Justine feels absolutely right.

"Now I know all your secrets," Justine says.

"Not quite."

Her eyebrows rise in surprise. "Oh?"

"You don't know my biggest one," I say, stopping to face her. Even totally alone it doesn't feel right saying it at full volume. Instead I press a kiss to her cheek before whispering in her ear. "I'm already falling in love with you."

The way she kisses me tells me that she is too.

14

JUSTINE

I couldn't have asked for a more perfect weekend. I'm sore from the sheer amount of sex and I feel like I'm glowing from being so close to Keenan. Getting to know him better and hearing his confession, I can't stop smiling.

It's still early, and I have clients this afternoon, but right now I feel like I'm bathing in perfect bliss, and I stretch out on my bed to take a glorious nap. There wasn't much sleep to be had last night.

I feel like I've barely closed my eyes when my phone starts to ring and I wake with a start, realizing that a couple of hours have passed. It's Morgan, but I'm not late yet. Probably something about the next protest. She was over the moon when she got the news that the plans to demolish the building were reversed.

"Hey Morgan," I say, answering. "What's up?"

"I need you at the Aster building right now. They're about to tear it down and we need bodies."

It feels like a bucket of ice water has been dumped over my head. "What? That's impossible. That was cancelled."

"I know that's what was said, but the bulldozers are here

and they're going to start with the park if we don't hold them off."

"Fuck. I'm on my way."

What the hell is happening? Keenan told me that he pulled the permits. It has to be a mistake. It *has* to be. This can't be happening again. Not again. There's probably still people in that building. But if they start with the park, the building won't be far behind. Not if they think they have the right to turn it down.

I throw on my shoes and grab what I need as quickly as I can before sprinting to my car. The drive isn't far, but every second counts. As soon as the car is on, I'm dialing Keenan. He has to know what's happening. But the phone goes straight to voicemail.

He went home, but I don't know if he fell asleep too or went to the office. It rolls over to voicemail and I don't bother to hide exactly how frantic I feel. "Keenan. They're demolishing. I don't know what happened but they're trying to take the park first. I'm going there now. Call me back."

I hang up and call him again immediately. Again, voicemail. Shit. If he doesn't know what's happening, he won't be able to stop it. But it has to be a mistake. They can't bulldoze without permits, right?

If they were bribed, they might not care. Dread sinks through my skin. Anyone can be bought. That's what I know. Anyone. For enough money you can be convinced not to care about people. People have problems, money solves those problems. That makes us all vulnerable.

Skidding around the corner, I nearly run my car onto the sidewalk. Morgan is right. The bulldozers are here and running, only being stopped by the thin line of people standing in front of them. They're blocking the patch of woods in the park.

A crowd is starting to gather, watching what's about to happen. I fling myself from the car, barely remembering to lock it before I'm tearing across the field toward the man in the suit who's clearly the one in charge. "What the hell are you doing? You have to stop. This is illegal!"

Every eye is on me now as I scream everything at the top of my lungs while I'm running. But that's good. If their eyes are on me, they're not on my friends.

I skid to a stop in front of the man. He's tall. Taller than Keenan and built thickly. Blond. And his mouth is twisted into a cruel smile. I've never met him before but that smile brings back memories all the same. That's the smile that does terrible things.

"And who, exactly, are you?" he asks, crossing his arms.

"It doesn't matter who I am. This demolition has no permits. It was cancelled and it's illegal. You need to take your machines off this property *now*."

He scoffs. "I *own* this property, and I can do as I damn well please."

"Tell that to the permits department and get the fuck out of here."

Victory shines in his eyes, and he pulls papers out from the inside pocket of his jacket. "Like I was showing your equally bitchy friend before she set up that line, seems like you've got your facts wrong."

The papers he hands me are demolition permits. Signed and dated by the city on Friday. For this address. Oh, fuck.

The man in front of me starts to laugh. "I think I know who you are," he says. "You're Keenan's activist slut. I don't know what kind of magic pussy you think you have, but this was always the plan. This project is way too profitable, and as you can see, the permits are legal. So stop pretending you're willing to die for a few trees and go try to fuck your way into someone else's profits, okay?"

Turning, he grabs a bullhorn from a nearby man in a hardhat. "Listen up," he says, voice echoing over the park. "We are going to move these bulldozers in ten seconds. We have legal permits. Now *move*."

To my horror, my friends do. They start to move away from the machines that are revving their engines. He starts to count down over the bullhorn, and I have a split-second to make a decision. I drop the papers to the ground and run, plastering myself against a tree directly in front of the largest machine. They're not going to kill me. They wouldn't dare. Threats are all well and good, but no one wants to go to jail for murder.

"Move," he says over the bullhorn.

My voice will never be heard over the sound of the engines, so I just shake my head.

"Go ahead," he says, and terror grips me, but I don't move. I hold my ground. They're not going to kill me. I don't think.

"Face it, hippy chick, your boyfriend approved this. You really want to get pissed at someone, it should be him."

Adrenaline is singing in my veins as the machines move towards me, the giant scoop lifting, and the tines stopping inches from my neck. I can't breathe. Keenan wouldn't have done this. He *wouldn't have*. I'm trying not to believe it, but the proof is right in front of me. The only thing that's keeping me from the dread is the humming of the engines and the sharp tines pointed at my throat.

"Are you going to move?"

I shake my head again. There are witnesses here. They're not going to impale me. But looking up at the man who's driving that bulldozer, I don't feel as sure as I would like to.

Across the field, I see a shining streak, and a car skids up onto the sidewalk next to mind. Keenan is running across the field at full speed; he's nearly a blur. The glimpse that I get of his face clears any doubt from my mind that he had anything to do with this.

His expression is pure rage. An avenging angel tearing toward the blond man. The asshole barely has time to see it coming before Keenan's fist connects with his jaw and he goes down.

The bullhorn falls to the side, and I can't hear anything they're saying over the roar, but I can see that Keenan is yelling at him. The blond takes a swing at him, but he ducks easily and puts him down again. In a second Keenan has the bullhorn to his lips. "Back the fuck up. Now."

It takes a second for them to engage, but slowly, the tines pull away from me, and I realize how badly I'm shaking and how pure adrenaline was keeping me standing.

Keenan reaches me a second before my knees give out, and he's holding me up now, crushing me to his chest. "Fuck, Justine."

I hold on to him, loving his strength and so grateful that he's here, and that I was right. That he had nothing to do with this. Any of it.

"I got your message," he says, suddenly audible as the engines retreat. "I came as fast as I could." Nervous laughter. "Am I going to have to keep saving your life?"

"Hopefully not," I say, digging my fingers into the fabric of his shirt. "But if I'm in danger, you're the one that I want to save me."

Keenan leans me back against the tree and kisses me hard. His fear and relief leak through, and there's something stirring in my gut that tells me this is deeper than anything I can imagine.

"What happened?" I asked. "Who is he?"

His face turns to stone. "That's Brandon Blake."

"As in Silverman & Blake."

"Yes. I told him I was cancelling the permits before we left on our trip. He was pissed, and I didn't care. He called the city and had them reinstated after I left the office. But I just fired him."

I gasp. "Can you do that?"

"I can," he says. "Human endangerment and going behind both my back and the board's? I can't imagine that that vote wouldn't be unanimous."

I lean my head forward on his chest. "Thank you for coming for me."

Keenan lifts my eyes back to his with his palm, letting it rest against my cheek. "I will always come for you, Justine. Always."

He kisses me, a soft press of lips that turns fierce. Far too fierce for the middle of a park. When he pulls away, I'm breathless and wanting. I don't think I'll ever truly have enough of him.

"I've got a secret," I tell him.

He grins. "You've already got all of mine. I'd love to hear one of yours."

My heart pounds in my chest. "I love you."

That grin goes wider, and he pulls me against him in a fierce hug. "That's the best secret you could have told me. I love you too."

EPILOGUE
JUSTINE

<u>Six Months Later</u>

The new headquarters for Delovery are amazing, and I don't think I'll ever get over how beautiful they are. Or the fact that they only exist because of Keenan. Silverman & Blake—now just Silverman Industries—has completely pivoted from commercial work for profit and is now geared toward renovating properties for vulnerable communities. The first thing he wanted to do when he saw the offices was to renovate them. In fact, the look of horror on his face when he walked in was utterly priceless.

But now the food pantry is wide and open, and it always feels happy.

Right now we're here gathering our groceries to take to Rose together. I've roped him into coming to meet my clients when he has the time, and Rose now likes my boyfriend more than she likes me. When she saw him for the first time, she looked him up and down, nodded, and said, "If I had been you, I would have fucked him too. Come on in."

I just about died from embarrassment, but Keenan couldn't stop laughing.

Morgan waves to us on the way out to her last client, and I wave back before the door shuts and we're alone. "I thought that she would never leave," I say.

For a second Keenan looks shocked. "You love Morgan. Did something happen?"

"Morgan is fine, but I needed to be alone with you." I grab his hand and pull him into the enclosed pantry. The dimness is perfect for what I have planned. "We've barely had any time this week, and I *need you*."

I pull him against me, already unbuckling his belt.

"You can't wait until we get home?" he asks with a laugh.

"You really want me to go to meet Rose so horny that I can barely look at you without wanting to lick your cock?"

Keenan grins. Excellent point. His mouth falls on mine, and I let out a moan. We've both been so busy this week that at the end of each day we've collapsed into bed together exhausted. But I need him like I need to breathe, and this has been our first opportunity in days.

"One second," Keenan says, pulling back.

"Keenan," I whine, "I need you to fuck me."

I love watching his eyes darken when I say things like that. "Believe me," he says, "I want to fuck you. But I have something for you first."

For a moment I'm about to say something snarky about what could possibly be more important than getting him inside me, but all of those words are taken away when he sinks down onto one knee. "Justine," he says.

"Holy shit."

"I thought about doing this my way. The grand way with

all the trappings, but I wasn't sure that you'd want that. So I decided that I'd look for the perfect moment. And this is it."

I laugh, tears suddenly flooding my eyes. "Is it?"

"We're together because of our chemistry. Because despite our differences and our assumptions about each other, we were drawn together, and we're better for it. Together. So here, now, doing what we love, this place feels perfect. I want to fuck you, Justine. But I want to fuck my fiancée even more. Will you marry me?"

"Yes." The word is choked with unshed tears, and I barely see the ring that he puts on my finger. It's shiny and beautiful and perfect. He's perfect too, lifting me up off my feet and pressing me against the wall so I can wrap my legs around his hips.

"You caught me by surprise," he says. "I don't have any condoms."

"Fuck the condoms," I say. "I just want you."

My hands are shaking as I get his belt undone and guide him home, savoring the delicious heat of him entering me slowly. We groan together, and there's nothing I think could be better than feeling him like this for the first time after saying yes.

The friction as he rocks his hips is new, and I'm already so wet that he has me on the edge of pleasure. "You feel so fucking good," he growls against my lips.

"More." That's the only word I have.

He gives it to me, unleashing all of that passion that he has to hold back. Keenan fucks me into the wall and it's good that no one is here. There's no chance that everyone in the whole building wouldn't hear me screaming his name.

Reaching between us, he finds my clit, adding fuel to the fire, and I can't hold myself back. Pent up arousal pours into my orgasm, and suddenly I'm in freefall. Stunning, perfect ecstasy that carries me and brings me back to him just as he comes. Heat filling me up.

This man is mine. I get this. Forever.

I've never felt so lucky, and I'll never be able to repay Lila for catching that fucking cold.

"I love you," I manage to say while I try to catch my breath.

"I think there's a chance," he says with a grin, "that I might love you more."